Beacon Hills High

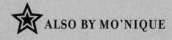 **ALSO BY MO'NIQUE**

Skinny Women Are Evil

Skinny Cooks Can't Be Trusted

H

Beacon Hills High

Mo'Nique

with **Sherri McGee McCovey**

Amistad

An Imprint of HarperCollinsPublishers

BEACON HILLS HIGH. Copyright © 2008 by Mo'Nique Hicks and Sherri
McGee McCovey. All rights reserved. Printed in the United States of
America. No part of this book may be used or reproduced in any man-
ner whatsoever without written permission except in the case of brief
quotations embodied in critical articles and reviews. For information
address HarperCollins Publishers, 10 East 53rd Street, New York, NY
10022.

HarperCollins books may be purchased for educational, business, or
sales promotional use. For information please write: Special Markets
Department, HarperCollins Publishers, 10 East 53rd Street, New York,
NY 10022.

FIRST EDITION

Designed by Judith Stagnitto Abbate / Abbate Design

Library of Congress Cataloging-in-Publication Data has been applied for.

ISBN 978-0-06-112106-7

08 09 10 11 12   OV/RRD   10 9 8 7 6 5 4 3 2 1

To All the Chunky Girls Who Believe, Like Eboni, That You Are Beautiful—Keep on Soaring. The Sky Is Not the Limit!

Beacon Hills High

Chapter 1

Open it, girl. Hurry up!" my best friend, Michelle, urges as I pick up the beige envelope on the kitchen counter with my name, Eboni Michelle Imes, typed neatly.

Is it good news or bad?

It had been two months since I carefully filled out and mailed off my application to Millwood. Now, the answer was finally here—an acceptance or rejection—to the tightest school in the city. Millwood is *the* most popular school in Baltimore, Maryland. The football team, the Mustangs, is the toughest. The basketball team has won the city championships five years straight, and even had a point guard who went directly to the NBA right after his senior year. Of course, the fine boys on these teams are a nice attraction, but also academically, Millwood grads go on to do big things. I'm about doing big things with my life. I want to be famous.

For some reason, though, today didn't feel like an acceptance-letter kind of day as Michelle and I walked home from school. It was gloomy, overcast. You know, one of those dreary days when all you wanna do is stay in the house under a mountain of blankets and zone out, or watch a marathon of MTV's *Real World*. Hotties in a phat crib make me think of my other favorite show, *Cribs*. These phat pads are always lavish. I imagine a crew rollin' up to film me in mine someday.

Back to reality.

"I need a snack first," I announce, laying my backpack down on the antique oak bench that had been in our family for generations, and head for the kitchen.

"Right behind you, E," Michelle says, setting hers down, too.

I look around and notice the sign DON'T MESS UP MARY'S KITCHEN next to my mother's favorite glass angels resting on the windowsill. My family has eaten so many good meals in this kitchen. I notice a package of pork chops Mom had taken out for dinner, thawing in the sink. I hope Mom will also hook up her slammin' three-cheese macaroni and cheese, string beans, and salad. That's one of my favorite meals.

"Is that one of your mama's sock-it-to-me cakes?" Michelle asks, eyeing the perfect yellow Bundt cake dripping with icing under a glass dome.

"Yep."

"Looks like we've found our afternoon snack," she quips. "So, get to cuttin'. And make sure you cut me a big piece."

Mom's sweets are legendary, especially her sock-it-to-me and 7-Up cakes. She doesn't make them often, but when she does, it's every man for himself in our house. People tell her all the time she should open a dessert shop. Her desserts are just that good. "Grab two plates," I instruct, snatching a knife from the drawer.

"How can you be so calm about the letter?"

"I've waited this long. What's another few minutes?"

"Did you finish your announcements?" Michelle asks, eyeing the box of blue-and-gold graduation cards sitting on the counter, which Mom and I had started addressing.

"Yep." I grin, picking one up and inspecting the fancy script.

It is real. In one week, I will be graduating.

"So, how do you think you did on the Spanish final?" Michelle asks, downing a glass of milk.

"Bien, mi amiga. Y tú?"

"Don't ask," she groans, breaking my conversational flow.

"My other finals were crazy, though," I share.

Thankfully, that is all behind me now. The only thing left to do is pick up my cap and gown and finalize the guest list for the graduation party Michelle and I are having in my backyard. "I can't wait to get to Millwood," Michelle says, trying to turn the conversation back to the letter.

"What if I didn't get in?"

"Well, the only way to know for sure is to open the letter," she presses.

I glance over at it again. "I hate this feeling."

"You got in, Eboni," my girl assures me with a smile. "I just know it."

Michelle Adams has been my best friend since our first day at Stanley Elementary School. I noticed her because we had on the exact same red-and-green plaid dresses, except she wore white tights with hers. Her hair was braided in two neat pigtails that touched her shoulders and were decorated with red ribbons.

Her round face and almond-shaped eyes made her look part Asian, but she was a sistah through and through. Unlike me, who cried when Mom waved good-bye, Michelle was excited to be at school. She walked over, put her arm around me, and said, "Don't cry." Then she told me how much she liked my dress. That made me laugh and before I knew it, we were playing on the monkey bars together. People thought we were sisters, and from that day, she'd been like a sister, getting me into—and out of—all sorts of trouble. In addition to matching outfits, we also shared the name Michelle. It was her first and my middle name. 'Chelle, as I called her, always had my back and I had hers.

Like in fourth grade, when the bully Madeline Osbourne told the whole school I had a crush on Kevin Kelly. Michelle got her straight for me. And the time in sixth grade, when I couldn't find anything to wear to the spring dance, she suggested the store where I found the perfect outfit—the only one left in my size.

For us, it has been one adventure after another, like the summer our class went to Great Adventure and we got left behind. We had met two high school boys from New Jersey in the line for a ride and we were too busy riding the roller coaster with them. We were feelin' real grown up until we got left at the park and had to call my older brother, Corey, to pick us up. He wasn't too happy about the three-hour drive, but we giggled all the way home and kept looking at the pictures we took kissing the boys in the photo booth.

There was also the time we got caught hangin' out at a high school party. Michelle's mom busted in the party and embarrassed us by dragging us out. We both got long restrictions for that one.

"Well, E, if you get in, the crew will be complete," Michelle says.

Our other girlfriends, Charisse and Yolanda, had already gotten their acceptance letters. To try to ensure my place, I included a heartfelt essay with my application, explaining why I'd be an ideal student. Everything, from being student-body historian and participating in junior band at Saddleback to being voted "Most Likely to Succeed" and organizing one of the tightest senior dances, was in the essay.

"Eboni, what's up? You've always been fearless. You're funny, everybody thinks you're mad cool, you're popular, and you probably get better grades than all of us, except Yolanda. Nobody gets better grades than that girl. Why wouldn't Millwood accept you?"

Michelle was right. We did run things at Saddleback. By "we" I mean Michelle, Yolanda, Charisse, and me—the Too Tight Crew (TTC). Each of us had our thing. Michelle was the enforcer. If some craziness jumped off, she handled things for us. Charisse was the frail beauty. Whenever she was overwhelmed, girlfriend got the shakes and there was nothing any of us could do to stop it. The brains of the group was Yolanda. She didn't seem to study hard but always got straight As. Though she was levelheaded, if necessary, Yo Yo would scrap right alongside Michelle. They called me "fashionista," because I loved to flip through the pages of *Essence* and *Ebony*, the magazine my parents named me after, and copy the fashions of the models.

Though I studied hard, I was an average student, and that was what worried me. But the Millwood application stated the decision wasn't based solely on grades. Hopefully, my extracurricular activities and family's history with the school would help.

"You're right," I say, snapping out of my funk. "It's time to do for Millwood what we've done at Saddleback. Run things," I say, psyching myself up.

"Exactly. Now quit trippin' and open it."

"Okay, okay." I walk over, pick up the envelope, tear it open, and focus on the first few lines.

"Well?" Michelle asks, hovering nearby. "What does it say?"

Dear Miss Imes,
Congratulations! You've been accepted to Millwood High
School. We are pleased that you'll be joining us for the up-
coming school year . . .

"I got in," I scream, grabbing my girl for a celebratory hug.

"Told you, E." Michelle beams.

"We're going to Mill-wood, we're goin' to Mill-wood," I chant, doing a happy dance around the kitchen.

It takes a minute for the good news to sink in, and when it does, I remember to give praise to the Man Upstairs. *Thanks, God, for hookin' a sistah up.*

"Okay girl, so where to first, Bebe or Gap?" Michelle grins from ear to ear.

"Didn't you already hit the mall?"

"And your point is?"

"That you got your gear for the new school year already," I reply.

"I'm going with you," she says slyly. "You might need help."

"Yeah, right."

"Though Beyoncé did have this dope Rocawear jumpsuit on I must find."

"To running things," I say, lifting my glass of milk for a celebratory toast.

"To the future." She smiles, grabbing a second slice of cake.

"Hey. What are you doing?"

"I'm taking this one home," she says, wrapping it up in a napkin. "My mama doesn't do cakes and I don't know when I'll get another piece."

"Okay, now on to the party. It's gotta be on and poppin'."

"I know." Michelle grins. "And we've gotta look fly as hell."

"No doubt." I raise my hand for a high five. "After all, we're high school women now."

That night, I can't sleep, thinking about all the exciting changes in my life and what it all means. Whenever things get to be crazy, happy, sad, or hectic, I always take time to talk to God. I learned about Him from my favorite grandmother, Mimmie, who introduced me to the "Man Upstairs," as she used to call Him, when I was eight.

One day, I heard her say, "Lord, help me," and asked whom she was talking to. She said, "Baby, I'm talking to the only one, no matter what I'm going through, who can make it better." She explained to me that I could call on Him, too. I loved Mimmie so much. She was so much fun and very wise, so, if she told me I could talk to someone to help me understand life, I believed her and I started to follow her advice and ask Him to help me figure things out.

Like the time Michelle got the crew into a fight with Saddleback's bully Latisha Swinton. I didn't want to fight her, but I knew I had to support my girl. After I had a talk with the Man Upstairs, Latisha and her crew were nowhere to be found when the after-school bell rang. I also called on Him to give me a sign that would let me know if the cutie Tony Wilcox was feelin' me. Two hours later, I couldn't believe it when he was standing in front of my locker helping me get it unstuck. God also answered my prayers when Corey had a close call in a motorcycle accident.

For me, the Man Upstairs always had a way of working things out, and He had worked out the acceptance beautifully.

Dear God,

Hey there. Well, like Mimmie used to say, "If you have a problem, take it to the Lord in prayer." Well, it's not a problem, more like a thank you and a good lookin' out on the acceptance to Millwood. I was a little nervous there for a second but it all worked out. I can't wait to get there. I can't wait to get to high school. I can't wait to start driving; to start dating. Right now, though, I've got a lot to do before the party Saturday. I love my life. And I love you, God.

Chapter 2

Security Square Mall was the Saturday hot spot. The place to see and be seen for just about everybody. Michelle and I were usually there every Saturday, especially since our girl Charisse worked at Gap.

"Dang, Security Square is on point today," I say to Michelle when we enter. "It seems even more crowded than usual and it's only ten o'clock."

"I know. Guess everybody is hangin' out now that school is over."

"I love it," I say, checking out all the shoppers milling about.

"All right ladies and gents, brothers and sistahs, don't forget to stop by and fill out an entry form for a chance to win this spankin' brand-new Cadillac Escalade. Fully loaded." Sunny Andre of KMAS-FM, Baltimore's hip-hop radio station, is set up for a live broadcast and spinnin' all the latest jams.

"Okay," I say, checking out the pearl-white Caddy. "I love that car."

"Wouldn't we look tight rollin' to school in that?"

"Heck, yeah." I laugh. "With some Beyoncé on blast."

"I can't wait to get my driver's license. That's the first class I'm signing up for," Michelle says.

"So, where to first?" I ask, ready to do some serious retail therapy.

"This is your shopping spree. I'm just along for the ride."

"You mean to tell me if you see somethin' tight you aren't gonna cop it?"

"Maybe." Michelle smirks.

"That's what I thought. Okay, let's hit Gap first. And remember you're the one who suggested we go shopping," I remind her.

"That graduation cash definitely comes in handy, doesn't it?"

"Heck, yeah and it's burning a hole in my purse," I share.

Fashion is my passion, but I wouldn't call myself a shopaholic, just a sistah who loves to always look nice. As a thick thirteen, I've managed to do okay despite designers who assume fluffy girls aren't interested in fly gear that showcases our figures. Sometimes it means designing my own looks. Once, I ripped the legs of a pair of jeans apart and redesigned it into a funky jean skirt. It came out so good, I ended up doing some for the crew. Soon everybody was trying to bite our style, so I decided to design more and sold them.

"Okay, girl, Operation 'Get Party Pretty' is in full effect," Michelle states. "And there's only one condition."

"What's that?" I ask.

"Everything's gotta grab our curves just right."

"No doubt."

"What're you thinking about wearing?"

"I don't know yet. But I'll know it when I see it," I say, still on the fence about my party look.

"There's your favorite store," my girl jokes as we pass Victoria's Secret. I haven't been back in there after Mom caught me sportin' a thong. I didn't think it was a big deal, since most of the girls at Saddleback wore them, but trying to explain to my mother that thongs are what you're supposed to wear with low-rise jeans, not big ole granny pant-ies, sparked a whole other conversation about why I didn't need to be wearing low-rise jeans, so I just decided to leave that subject—and the thongs—alone.

"I'd kill for a Caramel Frappuccino right about now," Michelle says as we approach the Starbucks kiosk.

"I'm right there with you, girlfriend."

I am so addicted to Caramel Frappuccinos that I have to have one every other day and keep a Starbucks card loaded with cash. "Maybe not," I say, eyeing the line wrapped around the corner. "I don't feel like waiting in that line."

"Yo, is that who I think it is?" Michelle slows down and zeros in.

"Where?"

"Five o'clock."

I turn just in time to see the crush of my life coming our way. *Damn, that boy is fine.*

I am madly in love with Vincent Williams. Big V is 6'6" and the star forward of the Millwood Marauders. His hand-some face is crowned by a head of thick, jet-black curls, his teeth are straight and white, and a dimple in the center of his chin is sexy as hell.

"What up, ladies?" He grins as he approaches with his crew, the Six-Footers. It's Michael "Big Mike" Newton, Brian Baskerville, and Gavin and Gordon Gray, known as the Twin Towers. They were hard to miss, proudly sportin' Millwood jerseys.

"Hey, guys," Michelle greets them. "What's up wit' y'all?"

"Chillin'," Vincent says before turning to me. "What's going on, E?"

"Hey," I say, feeling like a frog is suddenly lodged in my throat.

"Y'all gon' be at the party Saturday night, right?" Michelle asks.

"What party?" Big Mike says. "'Cause it ain't a party if we ain't in the house."

"Our graduation party." I find the words. I'm not about to let this opportunity pass if it means Vincent and I might finally connect.

"Yo, we didn't get no invites, did we, fellas?" Vincent turns to his boys, acting as if he's wounded by the omission.

"Nah," one of the Twin Towers grunts.

"Well, y'all are definitely invited, right, E?" Michelle says, eyeing Big Mike.

"Of course."

"We may roll through," Big Mike says, his eyes roaming the mall for girls. "Where's it at?"

"Eboni's house."

"Oh, all right then. How's Yvette doin'?" Mike asks, referring to my older sister.

"She's fine," I reply.

"Cool. Tell her I said, what's up."

"Sure."

"A'ight ladies. Peace out," Vincent finally chimes in as he rejoins the Twin Towers who're mackin' a set of identical twins.

"Peace," I say as my heart attempts to slow down and return to its normal pace.

Michelle exhales. "Wouldn't it be something if you ended up with Vincent and I ended up with Mike when we get to Millwood?"

"Yeah. And we'll have to beat all the haters off of us with a stick."

"You know I don't have a problem with that." Michelle smirks.

"Well, I do. I don't fight over boys, no matter how fine they are."

"You wouldn't fight for Vincent?"

"Nope."

Checking out a short jean dress at Gap suddenly gives me an idea. "Okay, I'm wearing a dress to the party."

"Seeing Vincent made you decide that?" Michelle asks, making a beeline to a rack of slinky tops.

"Yep. That boy inspires me," I say, looking for my size.

"Girl, you're crazy."

With a renewed mission to impress the hell out of Vincent, I get busy and attempt to put together a show-stopping look. "Did you see how he smiled at me?" I ask, browsing through a rack of jean dresses.

"Nope. I was too focused on Mike until he asked about Yvette," Michelle says disappointedly.

"Girl, you know Yvette's got a boyfriend. Trust me. She ain't thinking about Mike."

"Good. 'Cause I don't wanna have to fight your sister for my man, 'cause you know I will," she clowns.

"Whatever, 'Chelle."

The Gap is on point this day. One good thing is that our girl Charisse works at the store and we can always count on her to put some cute stuff aside for us. She immediately spots us when we walk through the door. "I'm so glad to see you guys, okay, we got a lot of cute stuff in yesterday, follow me," she says without even waiting for our response.

She grabs me by the hand and takes me on a dance throughout the store, moving fluidly from rack to rack, pulling off items in my size. She knows exactly what I like. At the end of our whirlwind, I purchase the boot-cut jeans I'd been wanting. I also scoop up a few T-shirts, a rhinestone-studded miniskirt, and a pair of silver hoop earrings and matching anklet. Charisse operates like my personal shopper.

Later, in Underground Station, Michelle finds the Roca-wear jumpsuit she had been dying for and a pair of sexy Steve Madden sandals. "This was definitely a good day," I say, counting my bags.

"Where to next?"

"The food court," I suggest.

"Right there with you, girl."

✳ ✳ ✳

Hey." Mom, Dad, Corey, and Yvette are all huddled in the living room when Michelle and I return from shopping. "What's going on? Why are y'all in here?"

"Looks like you girls did some damage at the mall," Mom observes. "Hope you didn't spend all of your graduation money in one day."

"I didn't," I assure her.

"Before you go to your room, come in and sit down," Daddy urges. "You too, Michelle. I've got some great news."

Perched in front of the fireplace, Daddy looks handsome in a navy blue pinstripe suit and his favorite red "power tie." "Well," he starts, eyeing each of us to ensure he has our full attention. "As you know, my real dream has always been to work for myself."

I glance at Mom, who's smiling like she's in on the secret, then at Corey, who's seven years older than me and a miniature version of Daddy, and Yvette, who just graduated from Millwood and is also engrossed in what our father is saying.

"Well, family, the dream has finally come true. After years of paperwork, interviews, flights back and forth to the corporate offices, and much prayer, our application for a McDonald's franchise has finally been approved."

"Ah, man. That's great, Dad." Corey jumps up for a high five.

"Yes!" I say, excited to see everybody so happy.

"Congratulations, Mr. Imes," Michelle adds.

"There's more," he continues.

"What, Daddy?" Yvette asks excitedly.

"Okay, family, are you ready for this," he says, looking around at everyone and pausing for dramatic effect.

"Tell us, Dad," Corey begs. "What?"

"It's in L.A."

"L.A.?" I scream, jumping up from the sofa.

"That's right, baby girl. We're movin' to Los Angeles."

Corey and Yvette look at each other in disbelief. "Good thing I applied to UCLA, too," Yvette chirps. "I better check on the status of my application."

"Oh snap. I can't believe we're really moving to Los Angeles. I can't wait." Corey jumps up happily.

Excited by their reactions, Mom goes to hug Daddy. I don't quite know what to do or say. Neither does Michelle. I suddenly feel light-headed, like I'm about to pass out. "I thought you all would be excited." Mom smiles.

All eyes then turn to me.

"Eboni," Dad says, waiting for my reaction. "Isn't that great news?"

"No," I protest. "I just got accepted to Millwood, remember?"

"Baby girl, all you've ever talked about is living in Los Angeles one day. I thought you'd be thrilled."

"That was before I got into Millwood," I moan, choking back tears. "I don't want to go now. I want to stay here with my friends." Daddy comes over and attempts to put his arm around me, but I turn away, not wanting anything to do with him. Right now, he's the enemy. I pick up my bags, motioning that I'm ready to leave the room.

"C'mon, Michelle," I say, feelin' a well of tears about to break.

"Honey, wait," Daddy says.

"John, let her go. She needs some time to process it all," Mom says. "She'll come around."

"Congratulations, Mr. and Mrs. Imes," Michelle offers.

"Thank you, Michelle," Daddy says. "Hopefully, you can convince Eboni."

"I'll try."

I fall on my bed and bury my head in my pillow. "I'm not going," I cry loudly. "I'm staying here with y'all."

"Don't cry, E," Michelle says, trying to console me.

"This is so jacked up," I moan.

Thinking of no more Baltimore, no more TTC, and no Millwood is unbearable. In one day, my life has gone from on point to what's the point.

"Here, girl," Michelle says, handing me a box of Kleenex. "Stop crying." I blow my nose so hard it makes my head throb. "Eboni, what's the one thing you've talked about since I've known you?"

"Blowin' up," I sniffle.

"Exactly. All you've ever talked about is how one day you're gonna go out to L.A. and become a big-time movie star," she reminds me. "Well, girl, looks like that day is here. You're on your way just like you predicted."

"True, but that was supposed to be later; after Millwood. If I wasn't supposed to go there, I wouldn't have gotten accepted, right?" I try to reason.

"Who knows? Maybe you're supposed to do something different and that something different is in L.A."

Ever since I watched reruns of the show *Moesha*, I've wanted to live in L.A. I had visions of being one of Mo's girlfriends, and smiling as photogs snapped pictures of me strolling along paparazzi-filled red carpets. Something about all eyes being on me was thrilling. I'd even perfected my signature for autographs, in case someone asked.

"You are so lucky," Michelle says sincerely. "I'd move to Cali in a heartbeat."

"Well then you go," I suggest, still trying to make sense of it all.

"Eboni, Hollywood is your dream, not mine. You gotta go out there and work it, girl," she urges. "Things happen for a reason."

"Well, what's the reason for this?"

"Only time will tell. But I'm telling you, if you go out there and run into my husband, T-Mac, you better tell him his wifey is on the way," Michelle teases, referring to our favorite R&B singer.

"Whatever," I sniff, crawling underneath my blanket, trying to wrap my mind around this U-turn in my life. T-Mac is the last thing on my mind. After hearing this news, six words are all that come to mind:

God . . . why hast Thou forsaken me?

Chapter 3

It had been a week since Dad dropped the L.A. bomb. I couldn't stop thinking about leaving all my friends. I still didn't quite know how I felt about it. Some days, I was mad. Other times the thought of really livin' in Cali seemed kinda cool. I imagined what it would be like having sunny weather all the time. What would I do with all my fly winter clothes? Sometimes I dreamed about being a celebrity, wearing the bomb sunglasses, slamming outfits, and driving around on the freeway in my convertible, a Mercedes-Benz, of course. That would have to wait, though. Tonight my focus is on our party.

If this is gonna be my last B-More Jam, it has to be a no-fuss affair, which means the dress I'd planned on has been replaced by a more comfortable two-piece jean suit, sneakers, and my favorite gold hoop earrings. My girl Marsha at Hair Affair had hooked me up with tight curls that took all day but it was worth it, because by party time, my hair would fall perfectly into place.

To prepare for the dual graduation/going-away jammie-jam, Dad and Mom went all out. Daddy has spent a fortune on crabs. He piled them up on one large table so people could get their grub on. Next to the table are the juicy hamburgers and plump hot dogs Dad has spent all day grilling. There is also a table with all the fixings: warm kaiser buns, mayonnaise, Dijon and honey mustard, relish, onions, cheese, and ketchup. We have bowls of chips and dip spread throughout the backyard. We have also hung two banners, one that says CONGRATULATIONS EBONI AND MICHELLE and another that says GOOD LUCK EBONI, WE'RE GONNA MISS YOU.

"Cheer up, E," Charisse urges when she sees me staring at the going-away sign. "You look too cute to be sad, and you don't want to look torn up when you-know-who shows up."

"You're right."

"Okay, it's official." Michelle beams, swooping by in an emerald green halter top and jeans. "This party is officially off the chain."

Everyone is in the house, including Saddleback brainiac Joey Robinson, partying alongside Angie Foster, who had been voted prettiest. Bad boy Larry North is there mackin' the school's "hot mama" April Valentine as Deejay Danno mixes all the latest jams.

"Ooh, that's my song right there," Michelle coos as she busts a move to the new Mary J. Blige cut and we squeeze onto the dance floor. That's when I feel a tap on my shoulder.

"Yo, E, check out who just walked in," Charisse leans in and whispers.

"Way ahead of you, girl," I say, glancing at Vincent, who looks fine in a black Sean John shirt and jeans as he makes his way through the crowd, gettin' brotherly pounds from all the fellas and admiring glances from all the girls. Vincent's presence makes this *the* party of the year. "Excuse me, Tony," I say to our class clown as I put my partying on pause. "My mom's calling me." He doesn't even slow down, he simply turns around and joins two other girls dancing next to us.

"Hey there."

"What up, gorgeous," Vincent greets me, checking out the festivities. "This looks like the spot."

"That's right."

"These are for you," he says, handing me the most amazing bouquet of flowers.

"Thanks. They're beautiful." I give him a big hug. *He smells so good to me.* Hopefully, all the girls see our exchange and realize they need to step off, 'cause old boy is mine; at least for tonight, anyway.

"You and your boys help yourselves to some food."

"Cool," he says, eyeing the endless spread. The Twin Towers waste no time diving into the table of buffalo wings, burgers, hot dogs, and chicken. But Vincent lingers a moment. "What's up with that?"

"What?" I ask, lost in Vincent-land.

"That." He points. I turn to see what he's talking about. "Oh that," I groan, acknowledging the going-away banner and snapping back to reality. "I've been trying to avoid it all night."

"Goin' somewhere?"

"We're moving to Los Angeles. My family's opening a McDonald's out there."

"Really? A Mickey D's, huh? That's tight. I'd love to kick it out in Cali."

"Really!" Suddenly I picture Vincent and me in L.A. together. I mean really, really together, as a couple. We would have a fancy house with a huge walk-in closet and a pool out back. I could see a whole bunch of his pro basketball teammates hobnobbing with my celebrity friends.

"Hell, yeah. There's a scout from SC coming to see me play this season. So, I gots to make sure my skills are on point," he informs me.

"Well, I'd rather stay here."

"Why?"

"Because I just got into Millwood."

"Girl, later for Millwood, Cali's the joint," he declares. "I got a cousin out there and he always be braggin' about all the fly honies."

That's not exactly the response I was hoping for, but nothing could ruin this night. "They aren't as fine as me," I brag.

"Oh, really." He grins. "Check you out."

"Yeah, check me out," I brag, turning around slowly so he can get a good look.

"Lovely," he observes, studying me from head to toe. Even though Vincent is a player and probably has just as much game off the court as he does on it, I still like him. He is cool and he makes me laugh.

"So when do you leave?"

"In a couple of weeks."

As we continue to talk, the music suddenly stops. I turn

to see Michelle, Charisse, and Yolanda standing by the dee-jay booth. "Eboni, could you please come up here," Michelle says. Everyone turns their attention to us as Mom and Dad come outside, holding a big cake.

"Well, girl, you know I love you like a sister," she says, putting her arm around me. "You've been my best friend and road dog since the second grade. Your peeps are like my own. I can't imagine going to Millwood without you. I'm gonna miss you, but I'll be out to Cali as soon as I save up enough money," she promises, wiping away tears. Everyone starts to clap and whistle. Michelle hugs me tight, then passes the microphone to Charisse.

"E, I still can't believe the TTC is breakin' up," she begins. "You're the one who always kept us together. And made us laugh with your crazy self. I wish I was goin' with you to Cali," Charisse shares. "Who am I gonna pull clothes for now?" Everybody hoots and hollers as Charisse hands the microphone over to Yolanda.

"Well, EI," Yolanda starts. "You know I'm not good at speeches, but I just want to tell you that I love you like a sister. And just so you don't forget about us, we want to give you this." She hands me a big pink shopping bag. I reach in and pull out a white T-shirt with the letters TTC WEST on the front and all of our names on the back.

"TTC lives on," she says, reaching in the bag and pulling out a framed photo of the four of us smiling in our graduation caps and gowns. "You'd better rep us well on the West Coast." Everyone whoops it up again as me and my girls form a group hug. Afterward, Yolanda passes the microphone to me. I manage to compose myself long enough to address my friends.

"Thank you guys for making this party so fun and special. I'm not quite sure what all of this means yet, or why my life has taken such a U-turn, but I want you all to know that I love you and I'm gonna miss you guys a lot." I direct my eyes in Vincent's direction. "Hold it down for me at Millwood and maybe, just maybe, if the Cali thing doesn't work out, I'll be back."

"All right, y'all, no more tears. This is a celebration. Babygirl, this one's for you," Deejay Danno says, kicking off a mix of West Coast tunes. First up is Biggie Smalls's "Goin' Back to Cali," followed by a mix of LL Cool J's version and Tupac's "California Love." Everyone goes wild on the dance floor. Corey runs over and snaps pictures with his digital camera of me with all of my friends. Though I hate for the evening to end, by midnight only a few people remain.

"Nice party, baby," Mom says, cleaning up and removing an empty platter from the table.

"Thanks, Mom. I had a ball."

"Well, you deserve it. You've worked hard."

I go back to mingle with the rest of my friends, including Vincent, who's talking to a couple of girls. "Hey, you. Great party."

"Thanks again for the flowers."

"You're welcome, Ma," he responds endearingly. "Well, I'm about to jet."

"I'll walk you out," I say, trying to be cool and casual, though I want to grab Vincent's face and tell him exactly how I feel about him, but what's the use? I am leaving. There is nothing I can do about this crush but let it burn, as one of my favorite singers, Usher, croons in his song of the same name. Vincent must've sensed my feelings, because all of a sudden his arm is around my shoulders.

"Well, E," he starts. "I know you're going out West. Just don't go out there and turn into one a them stuck-up Cali girls."

"Never," I swear, trying to prolong the moment. "Maybe we can e-mail or text each other sometime."

"That sounds cool, but I'm not real good with the e-mails, especially during the season. A brother's gotta focus."

"I understand," I say, disappointed by the dis.

"Well, girl, take care." He leans down and gives me a hug that makes me want to melt into his big, strong arms and never let go.

"You too," I whisper in his ear, basking in the musky smell of his cologne.

As our faces part, we look into each other's eyes and he smoothly goes in for something I dreamed about but still wasn't ready for—the kiss of a lifetime. *Oh my God, I can't believe I'm kissing Vincent Williams and he's got the softest lips.*

Dear God,
Whew! Tonight was great! It ended up being even better than I thought it would be. The highlight, of course, was kissing Vincent. Why did he finally come around, and how could he kiss me like that when he knows I have to go away? Boys. Why didn't You make them so we could understand them? I wanted him to feel bad about me leaving. Why couldn't he say, "Girl, I wish we could've

kicked it and gotten to know each other better"? Or, "You were always fine as hell and let's stay in touch and see if we can make something work"?

I'm still a little pissed about all this moving stuff, but I have no choice. I'm hoping You'll make the move to Cali cool. Make it fun. I guess I'm uneasy because there are just too many things I don't know about being out there. Who's gonna do my hair? What school am I gonna go to? Where are we gonna live? Who will my friends be? It just seems like so much to deal with. I know I'm supposed to trust You, but it would be much easier for all of us to just stay here in Baltimore. I hate to say this, but if the franchise thing somehow fell through, I wouldn't be mad about it. The only good thing about all of this, if there is such a thing, is that we're moving to Los Angeles instead of somewhere like Kentucky or Idaho. For that I am grateful. Good night!

Chapter 4

"*Knock knock*," Daddy says, sticking his head in my room.

"Hey, Daddy."

"You aren't still mad at me are you, baby girl?"

"No," I say, taking a break from packing. "I guess I'm just sad that I won't be able to go to school with Michelle and the girls."

"I know it's hard to leave your friends behind, but good friends are never far from us," Daddy declares. "If you ever want to invite the girls to L.A. for a visit, just let me know."

"Really?" I beam, excited for the first time in a long time.

"Really." He smiles. "I've racked up quite a few frequent flyer miles and I think I can spare a few if it means making you happy."

"Thanks, Daddy." I lean over, hug him tight, and give him a big kiss. "I can't wait to tell them." Then I kiss him again.

"Two kisses?"

"Yes, because I love you and appreciate everything you and Mom do for me even if I don't act like it sometimes."

"Well, that makes me feel good, baby girl." He smiles. "Real good." He stands up and looks around my cluttered mess of a room. "The movers will be here day after tomorrow and from the looks of things you've still got a lot of work to do in here."

"Don't remind me. Trying to pack up my entire life is hard."

"I know. Do your best. I'll let you get back to it."

The day of the big move seemed to come so fast, but I managed to get everything packed up in time for the movers to take it away.

"What up, E?" I hear as I bring my last bag out of the house. Michelle's brother, Lance, is parked in our driveway with the crew, who're along for the ride. He and Corey shoot the breeze as I talk to my girls.

"What's up, y'all?"

"How you feelin', girl?" 'Chelle asks.

"I'm cool."

"Is that all you're taking?" Yolanda gestures, noticing my small bag.

"Yep. I shipped all my other stuff. This is just for the plane and a few things to wear until my clothes get there."

"Well, I think that's everything," Daddy says, coming out to join us. "We better head for the airport before we miss our flight."

"Well, girl, take care of yourself," Michelle says, offering a final good-bye hug. "Love you."

"Love y'all, too."

"Oh, and like I told you before, if you run into T-Mac, you know what to do," Michelle reminds.

"Girl, if I see T-Mac, he's mine," I tease.

"Y'all can have T-Mac. Chris Brown is my baby's daddy." Charisse laughs.

"Oh, I almost forgot to tell y'all, Daddy said if you ever want to come out and visit, he'll take care of it."

"Seriously?" Charisse's eyes light up. "Cali? For real?"

"Yep."

"Well, you ain't said nuthin' but a word . . . we're there, then," Michelle assures me. "Maybe after first semester."

"Hello, girls," Mom says, joining our little sistahs' circle.

"Hello, Mrs. Imes," they reply in unison.

"Good luck at Millwood this year. Make us proud."

"We will," Charisse assures us.

"Well, we better roll. Freshman orientation is coming up and we've gotta go pick up our registration packets," Michelle informs me.

"To the TTC," I chant, unzipping my jacket to reveal the T-shirt they gave me at the party. "To the TTC," they chant back as they pile into Lance's Lexus and drive off.

On the way to Baltimore/Washington International, I gaze out at my hometown and try to remain positive. *L.A. is gonna be great . . . it's gonna be great . . . it's gonna be great.* Maybe if I say it enough, I'll start to believe it. After all, I am headed to the land of the stars and that's exactly what I plan to be in a few years, when I land my own show, anyway. I close my eyes and meditate on the moment.

> *Dear God,*
>
> *Thanks for giving me life; for loving me, and for my won-derful family and friends. Please help me to be positive about this move. Even though I seem cool with it, I'm struggling to be strong. Really, my heart is hurting and I don't know how to make it stop. I'm still confused, mad at times, and hurt that I won't be able to live here with people that I know and love. But I know You have a plan for me and I hold out hope that this is going to be all good.*

"How long is the flight again?" I ask no one in particular once we get to BWI.

"Five hours," Corey offers as he helps Daddy remove our bags from the car. The minute he found out about the move, he got on the computer and researched the flight route, year-round weather conditions, all of the main freeways, and the city's major attractions. He had also mapped out the way to UCLA, where Yvette would be attending college, and knew how far it was from our new house to our new restaurant. "It's actually six hours when you factor in weather conditions," he continues.

"Honey, why don't you and the girls go on in. We'll meet you at the gate," Daddy tells Mom. "Here's a few dollars to pick up whatever you want for the flight." He hands Yvette and me fifty-dollar bills.

I find the nearest newsstand and pick up my last bag of Utz potato chips, an assortment of puzzle books, *Sister 2 Sister*, and *Right On!* I notice T-Mac on the cover of *Teen People* and decide to grab it, too, so I can catch up on all the juicy L.A. gossip.

"That'll be twenty-five fifty," a scruffy teen announces. I hand him the crisp fifty.

"Need a bag?"

"Yes, please."

"So, where're you off to?" he asks, making small talk.

"Los Angeles."

"Ah, I'd kill to get out there and ride the California waves."

"You want my ticket?"

"I wish," he gushes. "And you can have my job."

Once we get to the gate, I observe all the people. Baltimoreans. My people.

"So, you feel better?" Yvette asks, turning to me.

"I guess," I lie.

Though we are only four years apart, Yvette and I are as different as night and day. She is the spitting image of Mom, petite, the color of a Hershey's Kiss and perfectly styled hair that falls just below her shoulders. Yvette looks like she belongs out West. For the flight, she has pulled together a faded pair of Baby Phat hip-hugger jeans, a tight white baby tee, and a sparkly pair of Steve Madden flats. Her makeup is flawless, and as usual her nails and feet are perfectly pampered. Both of our lives had been turned upside down, yet she managed to take it all in stride.

"Eboni, I know you think moving is the worst thing in the world, but you may find out that you like L.A. Consider it a new chapter in your life."

"Millwood would've been a great new chapter."

"Do you know how many people would kill to leave all this crazy Baltimore weather behind?" she continues. "I for one can't wait."

"That's because you don't have to leave all your friends behind."

"You don't think I'm gonna miss Kim, Camille, and Stacey?"

"Yeah, but they're all going away to college, too."

"So," she responds, closing her magazine. "Don't be afraid to expand your horizons. You'll make new friends. That's what I plan to do."

"Here you are, little ones," Daddy says, handing each of us boarding passes. When it's time to get on the plane, I'm the last one in line.

"Hello, what is your seat number?" a pretty flight attendant in a dark blue uniform asks as I make my way onboard.

"Three J," I reply, looking at my boarding pass.

"Right this way." She gestures toward the left side of the airplane.

"Is this first class?" I inquire.

"That's right." She smiles. "Welcome aboard."

I turn around, stunned. "Surprise, honey." Mom chuckles, clearly thrilled by my excitement.

"It costs a little bit more to go first class, but that's exactly where my girls should be; first class for my first-class family," Daddy crows proudly.

"Did you know about this?" I ask Yvette.

"Remember those new horizons I was telling you about? This is your new life, Eboni—first class."

"Alrighty then," I say, giddy. "We are big-ballin'." I find my seat, put my bag away, and settle into the big, cozy leather chair. It feels good, with my family trying to please me. How long can I work this?

"Good afternoon, my name is Maria and I'll be serving you today," a pretty Latina flight attendant greets us. "You're Miss Imes, right?" she asks, studying a piece of paper.

"Yes. But you can call me Eboni."

"That's a pretty name. I will do that, Miss Eboni. What would you like to drink before takeoff?"

"Do you have ginger ale?"

"Sure. Coming right up." She smiles.

Corey takes the seat next to me. Mom and Dad are directly behind us, and Yvette is across the aisle with a stack of UCLA brochures. "This is the only way to travel," Corey proclaims, breaking out an assortment of electronic gadgets.

"I don't want to miss a thing," I say, looking out of the window as the baggage handlers throw suitcases on a conveyor belt leading to the belly of the airplane.

"Here you are, Miss Eboni." Maria hands Corey and me glasses. I turn around to Mom and Dad and hold up my glass.

"Cheers."

They both hold up glasses of champagne. "To the new good life," Daddy toasts as he and Mom clink and sip.

I settle in and turn on my new iPod. In addition to T-Mac,

Usher, Beyoncé, and Alicia Keys, Corey has also downloaded a few songs from Danno's hot party mix. Up first is LL Cool J's "Goin' Back to Cali," which instantly transports me back to that night.

After takeoff, I pull out *Teen People* and read it from cover to cover, especially the article called "L.A.'s Hot Spots, Restaurants, and Spas." Before I can close my eyes and chill, Maria walks by and hands Corey and me cards.

"What's this?" I ask, opening it.

"A menu," Corey informs me.

"Okay, that's phat," I say, studying the selections.

"I'm havin' the filet mignon," he announces.

"I'll have the shrimp scampi," I reply, checking out the choices.

After a while, Maria brings us warm towels to wash our hands, more drinks, bowls of nuts, salads, our selected meal, and finally chocolate chip cookies and hot fudge sundaes. "Okay, I'm beyond stuffed," Corey informs me.

"Me too." I yawn. "Show me how to adjust my seat."

I push play on the Cali tunes playlist again as LL croons, ". . . I'm goin' back to Cali/stylin'/profilin'" . . . and imagine myself doing just that in a convertible Volkswagen Bug as I drift off to sleep.

It feels like only minutes have passed before I hear, "Ladies and gentlemen, we're about to make our approach into the Los Angeles area. Please bring your seat backs to the upright position. For those in first class with footrests, please adjust them at this time."

Corey nudges me. "We're about to land. Open the window."

I sit up, lift the shade, and look out at my new world. My iPod is still on the Cali tunes playlist, but this time, the old-school Bay Area trio known as Tony! Toni! Toné! are singing their hit "It Never Rains in Southern California." The smooth voice of lead singer, Raphael Saadiq, croons, " . . . maybe I'll take a flight out tonight/it never rains in Southern California/I'll see you when I get there . . ." Everything looks beautiful, except for a thin layer of brown stuff that seems to float below the clouds.

"Check out that smog," Corey informs me as he leans over to get a better look.

"What's smog?"

"It's a haze. It comes from too many cars," he schools me.

As the airplane gently descends, the transforming waters of the Pacific Ocean come into view and I imagine running along the beach like they do in the videos I've watched over and over again. A few minutes later, I notice objects moving along a stretch of highway. "That's the 405," Corey informs me, checking out the traffic. "It's one of the busiest freeways in the city."

The cars look like matchboxes as they inch along. To my left, I see the letters LAX flanked by six huge pillars that are all lit up in shades of red, blue, and green. "Check that out." I point so that Corey can see the glitzy-looking posts that seem to welcome us with magic.

"Ladies and gentlemen, we would like to be the first to welcome you to Los Angeles. If you'd like to reset your watch, the local time is 4:55 P.M."

That's the first adjustment—the three-hour time difference between Baltimore and Los Angeles.

Chapter 5

One thing you can't deny about Southern California is the weather. The day is bright, the air is dry, and the gentle breeze feels like we've just touched down on a tropical island. We were finally here. In the town where people flock to chase dreams. We were the Imes clan, L.A.'s newest dreamers.

"I wonder what's going on over there?" I ask, noticing a swarm of photographers.

"Looks like they're following someone," Corey observes.

The crowd moves closer. "Oh my God. It's LL Cool J," Yvette screams.

"Get your camera out. I'll take a picture for you." Yvette hands Daddy her camera and runs over to her favorite rapper.

"Excuse me," she says right before he gets into a stretch Hummer. "Can I please get a picture with you?"

"Sure," he responds, smiling and licking his lips.

"I love you so much. Your music is so dope."

"Love you, too, cutie." He winks as Daddy takes the picture. "Thanks."

"Thank you," Yvette gushes nervously. "Wait until my girls see this. They are gonna hate me."

"You're welcome." He grins as the photographers get a parting shot.

"Well, that was exciting." Daddy laughs. "I guess that's how it is out here. You see celebs everywhere."

"It sure was," Yvette says, checking out the photo. "This is going on my wall."

On the way to our new house, Daddy plays the proud tour guide. "What's the name of this street?" I ask, attempting to sound it out.

"Cen-ti-nel-a," Daddy replies phonetically.

"These sure are some crazy-sounding names," I say. "La Tijera, La Cienega, La Brea."

"They're Spanish," Corey schools us again. "We're close to Mexico. Even the name of the city is Spanish. Los Angeles means City of Angels."

I hope there are a few here assigned to me.

"That right there"—Daddy points—"is a Magic Johnson's T.G.I. Friday's restaurant and Starbucks."

"Wow." Corey looks on, impressed. "I wonder if he's ever there?"

"After the NBA, Magic Johnson built businesses in inner-city neighborhoods," Daddy notes.

"I heard on weekends people hang out, play chess, and they have poetry slams," Yvette chimes in.

"Does he own the Starbucks in Prince George's County?" I ask, remembering the face of a smiling black man on the wall.

"That's right," Daddy says. "The very same."

"Oh, I know who you're talkin' about. He's real tall."

"Duh," Yvette says. "He was a basketball player."

A few minutes later, we pass a corridor of oil wells and homes nestled in the hills.

"Finally, a street I can pronounce." I notice the sign STOCKER before we turn onto a street called Don Lorenzo.

"When your father first brought me to see the house, we got lost just trying to find our way out," laughs Mom.

"You'll get the hang of it," Daddy assures us. "It's the perfect location because we're only minutes from the airport, downtown, the beach, and the restaurant."

Dad turns the car onto yet another Don, this one called Don Carlos, and pulls into the driveway of a gray-and-white two-story Spanish-style house at the end of a cul-de-sac. "Well, gang, we're home," Daddy announces, unbuckling his seat belt.

"Wow," I say, impressed. "This is kinda dope."

We all get out of the car and gaze at the house. It's much larger than our house in Baltimore.

"I read that Baldwin Hills is located on a natural hilltop and named after Elias J. 'Lucky' Baldwin, a San Francisco hotelier and one of Los Angeles's wealthiest landowners and financiers," Corey informs us. "The winding streets all have names that begin with the Spanish word 'don,' which translates to 'sir' in English. For years, Baldwin Hills has been one of the city's hidden treasures."

"It sure looks beautiful," Yvette says.

"Most of the houses were built in the early 1950s. Ironically, the area shares the same initials—and a famous street, Rodeo—as Beverly Hills. The difference, though, is that the one in Baldwin Hills is pronounced RO-dee-o, while the one in Beverly Hills is pronounced Ro-DAY-o. Most of the homes have spectacular city views."

The entire family stares at Corey in amazement, allowing him to complete his monologue. When he's done, Yvette sucks her teeth and rolls her eyes. My parents smile as if they are sharing a private joke, then head toward the front door.

"You are too weird. What did you do, memorize that from some book?" I ask, with my hand on my hip. "You won't make friends this way." I shake my head.

Once inside, I run through the empty house to a sliding glass door and notice a kidney-shaped swimming pool with a slide. "We have a pool?"

"Surprise." Daddy grins. "And it's ready for you to jump right in."

"Can I?"

"There'll be plenty of time for that later," Mom says. "Right now, we've got to get the car unpacked."

"How many bedrooms?" I ask, looking around in awe.

"Four," Mom informs me.

"And I found mine," Yvette yells from upstairs.

"Hold up," I yell, charging up the wooden staircase. "Not so fast." I walk into the room across from Yvette's. "Wow, I can see palm trees," I tell Corey, looking out of my new bedroom window.

"They're everywhere." Yvette joins us, looking around. "So, is this you?"

"Yep."

Corey's room is next to mine, while Mom and Dad's room is on the first floor.

After unpacking, I can't take it any longer. Yvette, Corey, and I dive into our new pool.

Dear God,

We made it safely. Thanks. So far, L.A. seems cool. Our new house is definitely nicer than the one back home. I'm lovin' my new room and our fly new pool. I just hope it stays like this. It's already different from Baltimore. Instead of going to the park with the crew to swim, I can just put on my suit, open up the door, and go for a dip in my backyard. I love it! I just hope I love everything else. Well, I'm here. What's next?

Chapter 6

Welcome to the neighborhood, these are for you," I hear a strange voice say as I peek from upstairs.

"Thank you," Mom replies, accepting a large basket of pastries.

"I'm Linda Goldstein. This is my husband, Howard, and our daughter, Debra." A petite white woman with long black hair tucked neatly behind her ears introduces her family to us, reaching to shake Mom and Dad's hands. Weirdly, the mother and daughter seem to be the same size—maybe a five or six. "We're two houses down on the right."

"Why, hello. Don't you have a pretty face," the woman says to me when I enter the living room. "And what is your name?"

"Eboni."

"Nice to meet you, Eboni. This is our daughter, Debra."

"Hi," I greet them, confused by the fact that the Goldsteins are white and their daughter is African-American with smooth skin and long, wavy hair.

"Hi."

Debra looks like a true California girl—too skinny and smiley. She's wearing a chic peasant top and stonewashed capri jeans. She has an easy smile and the straightest, whitest teeth I've ever seen. "This is for you," she offers, handing me a small plant in a terra-cotta pot. "Welcome to Baldwin Hills."

"Thanks," I say, genuinely touched by the gift. "I'll put it in my new room."

"Well, if there's anything you need, please don't hesitate to call us," Linda continues, handing Mom a slip of paper. "These are all of our numbers."

"Thank you," Mom replies.

"I'd be happy to tell you the best places to eat and shop. You just name it."

"Do you play golf, John?" Howard asks Daddy.

"A little," Dad says, showing off an invisible swing. "Not as much as I'd like."

"Well, we'll have to get out on the course sometime. I belong to a great golf club. It's what I do when I'm not preparing for a case."

"Which is never," Mrs. Goldstein chimes in. "He's a workaholic."

"I've got to pay for all of the goodies my two girls like to enjoy." Mr. Goldstein chuckles happily. "They like nice things."

"So, how do you like L.A. so far?" Debra turns to me.

"So far, so good, but I haven't seen very much yet."

"Well, we'll have to change that."

"I've been working on my room, but it doesn't seem to be coming together. You wanna see?"

"Sure," she agrees. "Lead the way."

"Mom, we'll be back," I announce as we hightail it up to my room.

"So, where did you move from?" Debra asks, following me upstairs.

"Baltimore."

"Oh, like on that show, *The Wire*."

"Yep. But not that part of town. I had just gotten into the tightest school in the city," I add. "My girls and I were about to really run things and then my dad got a business here."

"Well," Debra says, "trust me, you'll be happy in a few months when we're chillin' in the sunshine instead of the snow."

"Well, here it is." I push open the door to my new world. "As you can see, it still needs a lot of work."

"Wow," she says, looking around. "This is a great space."

"You think so?"

"Yeah. You can do a lot with this room. I like the color you chose for the walls."

"Pink is my favorite color."

"What else do you want to do?" she asks.

"That's just it. I don't know."

"Well, what do you like?"

"Music. My favorite singers are T-Mac, Beyoncé, and Usher."

"Ooh, I love T-Mac, too." Her eyes light up. "Did you see him on the MTV Music Awards? I TiVo-ed it so I could watch it over and over again. I'm also all about Chris Brown and Zac Efron." She smiles. "They can dance their asses off."

"Yeah, they can." I laugh, not quite sure who Zac Efron is, and ask, "So, Debra, what do you think I should do in here?"

"Call me Deb. All my friends do," she offers.

"Okay, Deb."

"Well," she says, looking around again. "You could start by hookin' up the walls. There are some cool pullouts in the new *Teen Beat*. I've got a ton of them. I could bring some by if you'd like."

"That'd be cool, thanks," I say, getting a sudden burst of inspiration.

"So how are you fixed on the gadget front?"

"Excuse me?"

"You know, telephone, TV, TiVo, BlackBerry?"

"I talked my parents into my own phone and cable," I announce proudly.

"That's a good start. Try to see if they'll spring for a flat screen, too. It makes everything look so much better, especially when I'm watching *My Super Sweet Sixteen*, *America's Next Top Model*, and *College Hill*."

"I love *ANTM*, too," I shriek, referring to the initials of supermodel Tyra Banks's popular reality show.

"Which season was your favorite?"

"Cycle three with Tocarra. Girlfriend showed 'em how curvy girls work it," I scream as I slide my hands over my hips.

"She was all right." Deb turns up her lip, obviously not sharing my enthusiasm. "Eva the Diva was my girl. When she posed with that tarantula on her face, girlfriend was fierce," Deb snaps, using model lingo.

"Deb, honey, we better get going," Mrs. Goldstein shouts from downstairs.

"Well, I gotta run. My mom and I walk in the evenings.

Gotta keep the body tight." She smirks. "I'll give you my numbers."

"Okay," I say, offering a piece of paper and a pen.

"We can talk more later." She ignores the paper. "I'll just punch your digits into my cellie." She flips open a slim, chocolate-colored phone.

"We better get going. I've got a big case in the morning," Mr. Goldstein yells.

"So what else is new," Deb groans.

"Thanks again for the goodies." Mom smiles as she walks the Goldsteins to the door.

"Sure," Linda Goldstein says. "Enjoy."

"That woman sure can talk," Daddy says after they leave.

"But they seem nice," Mom replies, tacking the Goldsteins' information on the refrigerator.

"I wonder how Deb ended up with them?" I ask.

"Clearly, she's adopted," Mom says.

In my room, I lie back on the bed and gaze at the pretty fern in the terra-cotta pot.

Dear God,

I may have just met my first West Coast friend. She seems really cool. She also seems a lot older than me even though we're the same age. Thankfully, she's agreed to help me fix up my room. So far, so good!

Oh, and what's up with the parents? How does a black girl have white parents?

Chapter 7

It looks nice in here, honey," Mom observes as she checks on my room-decorating.

"Thanks. I'm almost finished." I step back to check out my handiwork.

Having a bigger room is cool, but trying to decorate it is hard. Since I missed home so much, Deb suggested I incorporate my life back in B-More with my new one in Cali. So far, there were framed photos of the TTC, one of Michelle and me at graduation, pictures of us from the party, and one that Charisse snuck and took of me and Vincent hugging. I even found a Maryland subway map and hung that on a wall.

To get me up on all the West Coast hot spots, Deb had hooked up a Hollywood Wall with people and places to visit: Venice Beach, Magic Mountain, Universal Studios, and Disneyland. The Hip-hop Wall of Fame was back, too, and filled with photos of my favorite rappers: T.I. with his sexy Southern swagger; dapper Jay-Z; Midwest's finest, Chingy and

Nelly; and last but not least, my favorite singer of all time, T-Mac.

Deb and I had hung out just about every day since the first day we met. It was cool to have someone nearby to help navigate the L.A. scene. Corey had also gotten my computer set up with a batch of funky screensavers. When I finally get online, there's an e-mail from Michelle.

From: Michellettc@aol.com
To: Ebonieyesttc@aol.com
Subject: Cali Update

Hey E,
What's up in L@L@? S@me ole thing here. Summer just isn't the same without you. We hung out at Dru Hill Park Sunday. Saw your boy Vincent mackin' some ugly girl. I also hung out with Big Mike. Girl, I am really feelin' him. I hope something jumps off this year when I get to the "Wood." Cl@sses start pretty soon. I've got five this semester, which is gonna kick my butt, but hey, this is high school, right? We knew we were gonna have to step it up. Hit me back when you aren't runnin' the streets with the celebs. I'm dyin' to hear all @bout your adventures in L@L@.

Peace and love,

M

TTC Rules

From: Ebonieyesttc@aol.com
To: Michellettc@aol.com
Re: Cali Update

Hey 'Chelle,
I can't believe it's been more than a month since we moved. So far, things are cool. The other day I was downtown with my mom and you aren't gonna believe who I saw . . . Rihanna. Girl, I almost died. She looked totally different than on TV. She was really short and thin. It seems like everybody out here is paper-thin. She was shopping with a posse of girls. I wanted to say something, but I didn't know what. I forgot to tell you when we first got here we ran into LL Cool J at the airport. Can you say fine. I thought Yvette was gonna lose her mind. It's wild bumpin' into famous people. Guess I'm gonna have to get used to the celeb thing, and you know I don't have a problem with that.

I'm still nervous about going to Crenshaw High. I don't know anything about it, except for the fact that it was the school Moesha, Hakeem, Kimmie, and Niecy attended on the show "Moesha." That's kinda exciting. Girl, everything out here is so different. There are so many cars. Fly ass cars, too. I'm talkin' about convertibles.

Girl, all of these adjustments—making new friends, learning my way around, going to a new school—are so complicated but I'm adjusting. From the looks of things, my B-More gear isn't gonna cut it in Cali. Everything from the gear to the way the girls wear their hair out here is different.

Wow, your class schedule sounds crazy. I don't register for another couple weeks. I can't believe Vincent was mackin' another girl. Nothing I can do about that now. So far, I haven't seen too many fine Cali guys.

Dang, I miss B-More. Dru Hill Park. And all of you guys. Tell the girls I said, "What's up." I'll hit you back again soon. Wish you were here!

Love,

E

Chapter 8

Well, *Mary*, Crenshaw is a fine school, but Beacon Hills is *the* top high school in the city," I overhear Mrs. Goldstein tell Mom as they plant hydrangeas in our backyard. "I'm sure Eboni would feel more comfortable if she and Deb were together."

"You're probably right," Mom agrees, hidden underneath a floppy straw hat. "It sounds wonderful."

"It is. They have a long tradition of academic excellence and produce forward thinkers. That's what you want for Eboni, right?"

"Yes, but Crenshaw is Eboni's home school. How would we get her in?"

"Don't worry about that. One of Howard's partners is on the board at Beacon Hills. I'm sure he can pull a few strings."

"Well, that's awfully kind of you," Mom says, offering Linda a glass of lemonade.

"See, I told you we might be able to go to school to-gether," Deb whispers as we eavesdrop on our mothers' conversation.

"I hope you're right."

"Of course I am," Deb insists. "My dad pretty much does anything I ask him to, and I asked him to hook you up so we can go to Beacon Hills together."

"Thanks for helping me."

"No problem. That's what friends are for. Okay, are you as addicted to this show as I am?" Deb asks, turning her attention to a fight going down on an MTV reality show, between a black girl from Louisiana and a gay white boy from New York. "There's always a fight."

"Yeah. Everybody's out of control. Sometimes it seems fake."

"You think so."

"I don't know. So, girl, where're the cool places to shop?"

"Melrose has got some pretty cool stuff. There's also Fred Segal. The Beverly Center is *the* joint, too. They've got all the hot stores like Abercrombie and Bebe. I can probably get my mom to take us Saturday."

"That would be cool."

All *right, girls*, buckle up," Mrs. Goldstein instructs as she puts her black Mercedes-Benz truck in drive and we set off for a day of pampering. "First stop, Contempo Nails."

"They do the best mani/pedis," Deb tells me as we turn onto a trendy street called Robertson. "Mom and I get them every week."

Clearly, being a Cali girl means maintaining regular beauty treatments. I can hear Vincent's words: *Don't go out there and turn into a Cali girl.* Too late. That's exactly what's happening. Contempo is the spot. When we arrive, every chair in the two-room shop is occupied with workers scrambling to service a steady stream of customers. "Hello Linda, Deb, and Deb's friend," the petite Korean owner, Diane, greets us. "Manicure pedicure?"

"Good morning, Diane. Yes. Three please," Mrs. Goldstein instructs.

"Okay," Diane replies, looking around. "You pick color."

"C'mon, E, they've got tons of shades." Deb leads me to a counter with a rainbow of polishes. "What color do you like?"

"I don't know, maybe a red or orange, with a couple of designs. What about you?"

"Oh, I always get Ballet Slipper," she says of the sheer white shade of polish. "Try it." I pick up a bottle and take it with me.

"We should get our eyebrows done, too," she suggests as we sit side by side in vibrating chairs while two young Korean girls work on our hands and feet.

"What's wrong with my eyebrows?"

"You mean besides the fact that they're bushy as hell?"

"Really?"

"Yes and you've got a mustache to match."

"I do not," I say, running my fingers over my top lip.

"I show you," the manicurist, Annie, cackles, holding up a mirror. "I remove. You look more pretty."

"C'mon, Eboni. Get a wax with me."

Before I know it, Deb has talked me into my first wax job. Back home, we weren't into all the plucking and waxing. That was another difference between here and B-More. I watch as Annie runs a wooden stick through a vat of thick hot wax that looks like golden honey, and then slathers it across my top lip and then places a white piece of gauze above my lip. I attempt to brace myself. "Oh my God . . . Oh my God . . . Oh my God," I repeat in nervous anticipation of the pain.

"Don't move," Annie scolds. "You make worse."

"Just hold on, Eboni." Deb grabs my hand for support. "It'll be over in a second."

I try to calm down and then feel a *riiiiiiiiipppp*. It takes a while for the sting to set in, and when it finally does, my face feels like it's on fire. "Omigod!" I jump up, scaring an old lady sitting beside me. "It burns."

"Oh, c'mon, Eboni. It's not that bad." Deb laughs.

"You're right. It's not bad. It's torture."

"If you think that's bad, wait until you get a Brazilian."

"What is a Brazilian?" I ask, still reeling from the lip wax.

"You've never heard of a Brazilian bikini wax?"

"No."

"It's when they wax all the hair off down there." She points between her legs. "I got my first one last summer. I loved it."

"You don't have to worry about me getting one of those."

"Well, if you ask me, you look better already," she says, leaning back in her chair so Annie can hook up her brows.

"Whatever," I say, unconvinced.

"Like they say, beauty is pain."

"Who's 'they'?" I ask, massaging my upper lip. "I bet *they* don't go through all this pluckin' and pullin'."

Annie hands me a mirror. I take a look and can't believe

totally clean. I never realized there was hair
ess it was because it's gone now.

_..., girls, let's hit it," Mrs. Goldstein says, wad-
dling in yellow paper shoes.

Back in the truck, we continue up Robertson and pass a
number of chic boutiques. "Okay, that's Kitson right there,"
Deb explains, pointing to a window filled with T-shirts and
shoes. "That's where Lindsay Lohan wrecked her car trying
to get away from the paparazzi and where Britney Spears and
Paris Hilton shop. They've got all kinds of adorable baby tees,
jeans, and shoes." We pull over and go into the store. There
isn't a lot of merchandise in there, just a few racks spread
throughout the store. It's as plush as some people's living
rooms, not overcrowded with clothes like the Gap. I walk up
to one of the three racks with T-shirts hanging. Deb is at my
side, and security is on my butt. As soon as I put my hand on
a hanger, a super-thin salesperson appears out of nowhere.
She's so thin that her hip bones seem to arrive before she
does. "May I help you with something?"

"Yes," I say. "Where are the large T-shirts like this
one?"

"Well," says the woman with the protruding hips. "We
only carry extra-smalls and smalls, and once in a while a
medium may sneak in." She giggles.

"So what you're telling me is that sixty percent of women
can't shop in this store?"

"What?" she says, confused.

"Sixty percent of women wear a size twelve or above." I
smile.

The saleswoman draws her eyebrows together as if she's in a fog. "So you are only selling to forty percent of the female population," I continue to school her.

"Not in L.A.," she chirps, completely missing my point.

"You should have a better attitude toward fly girls who aren't sticks, otherwise you may soon lose your job."

I feel Deb latch onto my hand and start to pull me out of the store. I look at her and see that Mrs. Goldstein is already in the car with the key in the ignition. We get into the car quietly. "I definitely wasn't feeling that spot," I break the silence.

Mrs. Goldstein speaks up, "Okay, up here on the left is the restaurant The Ivy. Everybody from Chris Rock to Nicole Ritchie lunches there."

"Why is that guy sitting there with that camera?"

"He's a paparazzo," Mrs. Goldstein explains. "They get paid millions for just the right photo of some celebrity. It's disgusting."

"That's wild." I notice a fat man angling his lens in the direction of outdoor diners. "Just for one picture."

"If it's the right shot of the right celebrity. I wonder who's there today," she says as we try to spot whoever is coming out.

I had visions of some paparazzo trying to catch T-Mac and me coming out of one of the trendy spots. Though I'd heard people talk about being chased by crazy photographers, it was a trip to be up close and personal with the craziness.

"Are you hungry?"

"Starved."

"Let's head over to Johnny Rockets, Mom," Deb suggests. "They've got the best burgers and shakes in town."

"Sounds good to me."

How'd *it go?*" Mom asks when we get home.

"Great," I lie.

My mother is mixing cornbread batter for dinner. "I hope you didn't get anything we're gonna have to return."

"No, ma'am. Is it okay if we go swimming for a little while before dinner?"

"Sure," Mom says as she pulls one of her sock-it-to-me cakes out of the oven.

"Smells good." Deb sniffs. "My mom hardly ever cooks."

"Really?"

"Yep. But it's cool with me because she's not a very good cook. We usually do takeout."

"Mom, can Deb stay for dinner?"

"Sure. There's plenty."

"Thanks for today. I love my nails and the wax is cool, too."

"Sure," she says as we spread towels out on two deck chairs. Mom had fixed the backyard up like a resort, with all kinds of furniture and a grill for Daddy.

"So are you excited about going to Beacon Hills?"

"Yeah. I'm even more happy about the fact that I'll know someone," I say. "I like your swimsuit."

"Thanks. I got it a few months ago from Old Navy," she

says of the red-white-and-blue bikini. "My mom bought me three of them, but this is my favorite one. It's real patriotic."

"I need a new swimsuit," I share, stretching out.

"They had tons of cute one-pieces."

"I want a bikini," I say. "Maybe one like yours."

"You'd rock a bikini?" Deb asks, rising from her chair.

"Sure. Why not?"

"I don't know," she says, lying back down. "I just thought. Never mind. You go, girl."

"Does it sound crazy that I'd sport a bikini?"

"Kinda."

"Why? Because I'm not a size zero?"

"I guess I'd be scared people would laugh."

"Trust me. I haven't had any complaints."

"Well, work it then, Miss E."

"I plan to."

After dinner, I head upstairs and experiment with a few new hairstyles. Deb had given me the number to her stylist, Red, at a salon called Mane Appearance. Like just about everything in L.A., Mane Appearance is one of those fly salons with bowls where they can shampoo your hair while you sit up. Red, a tall woman with shoulder-length hair and freckles, had an easygoing personality and laughed at everything I said. I wanted a weave, but since Mom wasn't feelin' the weave thing, Red gave me a cellophane and a press-n-curl that left my hair as soft as silk.

"Well, well, well," Daddy says, coming in to check me out. "I almost didn't recognize you."

"Yeah, right, Dad."

"So, the big day is coming up, huh?"

"Yep."

"How do you feel?"

"Okay, I guess."

"You look so grown-up," he compliments. "I like that outfit on you, honey."

"Thanks. But I'm still tryin' to decide," I tell him, not sure about my first-day-of-high-school look.

"I'm so glad I'm not a female." He laughs. "If you ask me, I say go with that one."

"You really think so?"

"Definitely," he urges, heading for the door. "That's the one."

From: Ebonieyesttc@aol.com
To: Michellettc@aol.com
Subject: Cali Update

Hey 'Chelle,
Got your last e-mail and the care package. Thanks for the Utz chips and Tastykakes. It was all right on time. The big day is coming up. It's still hard to believe I'm about to start my first day of high school without y'all. And in Cali of all places.

I thought it would be crazy trying to get settled here, but it's actually been pretty cool and I'm kinda excited.

Did I tell you that last Saturday Daddy and I were havin' breakfast at this slammin' spot called Roscoe's Chicken and Waffles and Ice Cube and his son were sitting in the booth next to us getting their grub on? Girl, I was buggin'. He's so much cuter in person than in all of his movies. Nice, too. He said "hi" when he noticed me staring. Then, last week Nick Cannon came into our McDonald's. I was trying to wait on him, but I didn't get there fast enough. He's really tall and skinny. Bumping into stars seems to be no big deal out here. It's still a big deal to me, though.

Well, girl, look out for your Cali care package. Hope you like it.

Love,

E

Chapter 9

Good *morning, L.A.,* welcome to Biiiig Boy's neighborhood. And what a beautiful day it is in the neighborhood," a voice buzzes from the sleek radio alarm clock next to my bed as the deejay Big Boy of Power 106 laughs at his morning crew's prank call to some unsuspecting person.

"Morning." I yawn, entering the kitchen for breakfast.

"Morning, sweetie," Mom greets me from her newspapers.

"Where is everybody?"

"Yvette called to wish you good luck on your first day."

Shortly after we arrived in L.A., Yvette was able to move into the dorms. She is having a ball adjusting to campus life, which means we hardly see her. "Daddy and Corey are already at the restaurant. Your father left a note for you on the dining-room table."

I go into the dining room, open up the letter, and find a crisp twenty-dollar bill tucked inside.

Good Morning, Honey,
Here's a little spending change for your first day. Hope it's
a good one.

Love, Daddy

I pocket the twenty, go back into the kitchen, and grab a plate. "So, how'd you sleep?" Mom asks, putting her cup in the sink.

"Good," I say, eyeing a big plate of French toast, scrambled eggs, and bacon. "This looks great."

"We need to leave in an hour, so you don't have a lot of time."

"I know. I still have to take a shower and figure out what I'm wearing."

"I thought you did all of that last night."

"I thought so, too, but now I'm not so sure." I stress, pouring a glass of orange juice.

You *look great,*" Deb gushes as she opens the car door and gets in, sportin' a fuchsia Baby Phat warm-up suit, her naturally curly hair parted down the middle.

"It took thirty minutes in front of the mirror to work this out," I say of the matching short ensemble I eventually settled on. "You look great, too."

"Thanks."

As Mom drives up Olympic, I start to get anxious. Twenty minutes later, we pull up in front of the campus. "Wow." I'm utterly amazed.

Beacon Hills's sprawling front lawn and tennis courts

are unbelievable. And just so you know exactly where you are, four marble blocks spell out BHHS. "What's that?" I point to a huge tower painted with flowers.

"It's an oil well," Deb tells me.

"Okay, that's tight. A school with an oil well and I go to it. Wait until I tell my girls back home about this. They aren't gonna believe it. Do any stars go to school here?"

"A few have graduated from here."

"Like who?"

"The singer Lenny Kravitz, the actor Nicholas Cage, and the rapper Romeo."

"Well, one thing's for sure," I say as Mom parks.

"What's that, honey?"

"I'm not in Baltimore anymore," I utter, noticing a group of students congregating on the lawn. Not far away from them a trio of boys in surfer shorts and T-shirts fly through the air on skateboards as two girls, decked out in tank tops, jeans, and matching Fendi backpacks pile out of a bright-yellow Hummer.

"Okay, Eboni, you ready to do this?" Deb asks.

"Yep," I say, psyching myself up. "Ready."

"Have a good day, girls."

"Thanks, Mom."

"Oh, and remember, if for some reason you have a problem, call me."

"Okay," I say, before turning to face the mighty Beacon Hills High.

"What's your first class?" I ask.

"I think I've got Spanish."

"Oh, looks like I've got English."

"Well, you wanna meet up for lunch?"

"Cool," I say. "As big as this school is, I hope I can find the cafeteria."

"You'll be fine, Eboni."

"You, too." I smile as we climb the stairs and go our separate ways.

Okay, God, You got me into this new-school mess. Now, I'm-a need You to get me through it.

Inside the large building, I discover a maze of hallways and corridors. When I finally find Freshman English, there's only one seat left and it's right in front. *Great.* As I attempt to sit in the tight seat, my backpack goes crashing to the floor. Before I can pick it up, a hand reaches down and passes it to me.

"Thanks," I say, glancing at a curly-haired boy.

"Don't mention it," he replies. "I'm Juan." He smiles while batting his eyelashes. He has a perfect set of matching dimples on either side of his face that look like they've been swiped with blush.

"Eboni."

"Like the magazine?"

"Yeah. But with an *i* instead of a *y.*"

"That's hot."

"Really?"

"That was the first magazine with people in it that looked like us back in P.R."

"What's P.R.?"

"Puerto Rico. Where I'm from."

"I've always wanted to go there."

"Trust me, honey, we're better off right here in the lap of friggin' luxury." Juan laughs.

"If you say so."

"Oh, I say so. Tell me what's better than L.A.?"

"M.D."

"What's M.D.?" He looks at me, puzzled.

"Maryland. That's where I'm from."

"Oh, that's where that accent is from."

"I don't have an accent. Y'all out here got the accents," I say defensively.

"Yeah, okay. If *y'all* say so," he mimics.

"Well, you West Coast folks dress funny," I tease, checking out Juan's extra-colorful preppy pink-and-green polo shirt with the collar turned up and matching argyle vest. He has on pink-and-green slacks and a pair of plastic slip-on shoes. Instead of the same color, he's sportin' one pink shoe and one green one.

"Welcome, class. My name is Mrs. Price," a matronly woman with wire-rimmed glasses that tip the bridge of her nose says as she turns and writes her name on the board. "This is Freshman English. I look forward to our time together this semester as we focus on classics such as Thoreau, Shakespeare, and Hemingway. We will read one book each week." *Okay, clearly this woman is insane. Who has time for that?* "Though it sounds quite daunting, trust me, once you begin to read the wonderful stories of these classic authors, you'll be just as hooked as I was when I discovered them years ago."

The class groans in unison. "Groan if you must. But please be respectful of this time and this place. Now, in my hand is the curriculum for the semester. Please take one and pass them along. After each book, there will be a report."

"Okay, am I crazy or is she?" I whisper to Juan as I flip through the lengthy syllabus. "This is the first class and already it's insane."

"Get used to it. This is BH, baby."

When the bell rings, the entire class jumps up. "Good day, ladies and gentlemen. I will see you bright and early to-morrow, and please arrive on time."

"What do you have next?" Juan asks, strapping on a backpack.

"Is that Gucci?"

"This old thing," he says. "Yeah. I got it last season."

"Well, excuse me. Let's see." I pull out my schedule. "Looks like biology."

"Me, too." He lights up. "With who?"

"Hale."

"Bummer. I've got some dude named Dean."

"You know the way to the Science Building?"

"We can get lost together." He laughs, shoving the crazy English schedule into a notebook.

"After you."

Every hallway is jam-packed as we stroll along a row of neat blue lockers and pass a brightly colored sign with the mantra INTEGRITY, RESPECT, AND RESPONSIBILITY STARTS WITH YOU. I realize people are staring but can't figure out if they're gawking at me or at Juan, who is sashaying down the hallway like he's a girl. "So, how long have you lived here?" I ask, continuing our small talk.

"Six years. We moved so that my mom could take care of my grandmother."

"Do you like it?"

"Yes, baby doll, but I'm on my way to FIT in New York after this."

"What's FIT?"

"The Fashion Institute of Technology," he informs me. "New York is all that. What about you?"

"I've been here a few months. My father got a job at McDonald's."

"Hold the phone. You moved here because your dad got a job working at McDonald's?"

"No, we own one," I clarify.

"Well, all right, then. That's fierce. Well, this looks like me," Juan announces as we approach a classroom. "Maybe I'll see you for a little chow at lunch."

"Great. I'm supposed to meet my friend Deb, too."

"Okay, then. Later, E."

"Hey, that's what my girls back home call me," I tell him, surprised to hear it here.

"Well, consider me your first West Coast girlfriend." He winks.

"Yeah, right. See you."

As I hustle to find my room, I lay eyes on the finest guy

since my Baltimore crush, Vincent. He's got skin the color of a Hershey's Kiss and a body that is so ripped it can't be contained by something as simple as a shirt. His close haircut is accented by diamond studs in each ear and an equally bling-ed out cross that thumps against his Beacon Hills football jersey. I can't help but stare. "Excuse me. You're blocking my locker." A wiry girl with freckles interrupts my gaze.

"Oh, sorry. My bad," I say, moving away, embarrassed. I glance back again and notice the name HICKS on the back of his jersey, and the back looks just as fine as the front.

"Hey, G," a Ciara look-alike purrs. She's a sistah with sandy-blond hair, but I can't tell if it's a wig, a weave, or her own. It's clear that she thinks she's all that, especially when she slinks up to Mr. Eye Candy in a pair of short shorts that show off her long, shapely legs.

"What up?" He winks.

Before I can bask in the fineness of this oh-so-sexy chocolate drop, the first bell rings, signaling I have three minutes to find my next class.

*E*boni." Deb waves from a table in the middle of the lunchroom.

"Hey." I sigh, setting an armload of books down on the table.

"Why didn't you put those in your locker?"

"Because I had to rush to my second and third periods. One was way out by the auditorium, and by the time it was over, I was so hungry I didn't feel like going all the way back to the other side of campus to find my locker and put them away."

"My locker's far, too. Guess that's what they do to freshmen. Next time, run up here for nutrition and grab something so you won't be so hungry."

"I'll have to remember that."

My class schedule is: Freshman English, Biology, nutrition, Spanish, Debate, lunch, then Algebra and gym. It's a pretty cool schedule once I get the hang of it.

At lunchtime, the cafeteria is like a mini–United Nations. In one corner, a group of Iranians are posted along a back wall just below windows that overlook the L.A. cityscape. In another area, a few Asian students sit together. There are also a number of Latin and African-American students sprinkled in the mix. In the middle of the crowd are the jocks, a rowdy, out of control bunch who are anxiously checkin' out the new crop of female students. Every time a girl enters, they hold up French fries to signify their rating on a scale from one to ten. "So, how's it going?" Deb asks.

"Good. But I can't believe how much homework I have already."

"Yeah, me, too."

"So, what's good to eat here?"

"Name it, they've got it," she says. "I just got a salad."

"Looks good but I'm gonna need more than that."

"Go check it out for yourself," she urges.

I notice a section called "The Salad Patch," where a line

of waifs are piling their plates up with salad fixings. At the
front of the line is the Ciara look-alike talking on a pink,
diamond-studded cell phone, pushing along a tray of carrots
and lettuce. Two girls who are obviously a part of her crew
are close behind her.

"That's what I won't be havin'," I hear a familiar voice
say.

"What?"

"I said, that's what I won't be havin'." Juan smirks nearby.
"Baby, lettuce is for bunnies."

"You're crazy," I tell him.

"It's the truth."

"Okay, well, point me to where I can get something that
looks and tastes good."

"Right this way, *señorita*." We head for another area,
called "The Grill," which is also crowded.

"Wha can I get choo?" a woman with a heavy Spanish
accent asks.

"Let me get a cheeseburger medium well with bacon,"
Juan orders.

"Chu want fries wit dat?" she inquires, flipping a patty
onto a grill.

"Yeah, lots of 'em."

"And choo, *chica*?" she says, turning to me.

"I'll have the same, but make mine well done with onion
rings."

"That's what I'm talkin' about, a girl who isn't afraid to
eat. I like that."

"I could say the same about you."

I rejoin Deb and introduce her to Juan. "Deb this is Juan. Juan, Deb."

"Nice to meet you," Deb says. "Pull up a chair."

"Looks like the new Baby Phat," he says, referring to Deb's outfit.

"It is indeed." She smiles. "Good eye."

"*Très* cute." Juan winks. "I know my designers."

"Did you go to El Rodeo?" Deb inquires.

"Yep," Juan replies, tearing open a packet of ketchup and squirting it on the side of his tray. "Only for a year, though."

"I thought your face looked familiar. Dang, you guys sure got a ton of food," Deb says, observing our plates.

"Help yourself," I say, pushing the tray her way.

"I'll just have one onion ring," she says, going for it.

"Baby, I'm as hungry as a hostage," Juan says, gobbling a few fries before noticing a cup on my tray. "Ohmigod. Is that ranch dressing?"

"Yeah, I love to dip my onion rings in it."

"Me, too," he says, dunking a couple of his fries in the thick white salad dressing.

As we get our grub on, the hottie from earlier enters. "Okay, who is that fine chocolate-y something right there?" I lean over and whisper to Deb. "I saw him on my way to second period. He's beautiful."

"Oh, that's Gene Hicks. He's quarterback of the Panthers. Everyone calls him G. Stand in line 'cause everybody wants some of that."

"I understand why," I say, caught up in a G Hicks trance.

"Me, too," Juan says, gazing right along with us. "Boyfriend has got some guns on him."

Deb and I look at each other and laugh. "Okay, you're funny, Juan."

"Yo, G," one of his teammates yells. "What's up?"

"Yo!" he greets his friends, making a beeline to the group and giving them love. "What's crackin' up in this piece?"

"Just checkin' out the new crop of honies," I overhear one of his boys say as an unsuspecting girl enters the cafeteria. "That would be a two," a short jock squeals as the others hold up their scores in fries.

"Yo, we were just about to jet out to the field," another jock informs G.

"Let's roll then," he says, adjusting his black mesh shorts so they'll hang low. "Let me just grab a burger real quick."

"Cool," another one crows as the jocks barrel toward the door. They stop in their tracks when an attractive group of girls, among them the Ciara look-alike, passes.

"Looks like boyfriend's got it bad." Juan smirks, noticing the exchange.

"What do you mean?"

"He's caught up in that Maya madness. Boyfriend nearly fell over when Blondie smiled at him." I turn around just in time to see the girl in the shorts take it one step further and blow G a kiss.

"That's Maya Williams." Deb offers us the lowdown. "She went to the middle school next to mine. She and her crew are a bunch of hoochie mamas."

"I've got math with her and everyone, including my teacher, was mesmerized when she walked in late," I fill them in.

"Well, hate to eat and run, but I gotta go," Juan informs us. "Yeah. Bright and early for that god-awful English class."

From: Ebonieyesttc@aol.com
To: Michellettc@aol.com
Re: Cali Update

Hey Girl,
The first day was cool. You should see this place. It's three times bigger than Millwood and just tryin' to find my classes is crazy. The cafeteria looks like a mini food court. The kids get dropped off in Range Rovers and some even drive them. I've got six classes: Freshman English is a trip. Get this . . . the teacher expects us to read a book every week. Biology, all I can say about that one is that I don't know how I'm gonna pass because we're supposed to dissect a frog. You know I don't do frogs—and I definitely don't do dissection. Algebra is gonna be interesting. The teacher promises that he's going to make math fun. There ain't nothin' fun about sitting through variables, expressions, and equations, but it's a requirement that I don't want to repeat, so I'm gonna have to give it my all. Spanish is gonna be intense. During the entire class we can't speak any English. Debate is probably gonna be my favorite. The teacher, Mr. Hinds, is cool as hell. Then there's gym, and this isn't your average gym. It's got a swimming pool underneath the floor! There's also a television station, a weekly newspaper, and a radio station, all on campus.

I have two friends, Deb and this boy named Juan Guerrero in Freshman English. Boyfriend is girlier than me, but he's cool. I also met a girl named Robin Smith who is in my Debate class. She reminds me a lot of you, except she's white and has bushy red hair. Well, that's the scoop from here. What're y'all up to?

Luv,

E

Chapter 10

By the end of the first week, I had mastered making it to class and my locker before the final bell. "Hey." I wave to Deb when I meet up with her at our usual lunch table.

"Hey."

"Are you okay?"

"Yeah. Just tired," she says, looking flushed.

"What's your next class?"

"Gym."

"And that's all you're eating." I notice a half-eaten little salad Deb has barely touched.

"I'm not really that hungry, anyway," she shares.

"I know, girl, but you really need to eat more than that."

"I ate during nutrition," Deb says. "I think I'll go on down and change into my gym clothes. See you at the bus stop."

"Yeah, see ya," I say, concerned about my friend.

* * *

Have *you ever thought* about going on a diet?" Deb suggests as we wait for the bus after school.

"I like food too much," I say, checkin' out two homeless men sleeping on a park bench. The only difference between the homeless here and back in Baltimore is that these homeless people look like with a little soap and water they could star in their own television show.

"I think I'm gonna try this one I read about in *Us Weekly.* Jessica Simpson lost eight pounds in two weeks," Deb announces. "I figure if I do it a month, I can lose at least fifteen."

"Those magazines are crazy," I tell her. "Most of the stories are fake and so are the pictures of the skinny women in them."

"No they aren't," she protests.

"Yes they are," I counter. "I saw an episode of *Tyra* where she talked about how magazines change the way celebrities look all the time. They even did it to her. She held up a photo and showed how she looked before they airbrushed it to make her look thinner. It's all an illusion."

"I've seen her in person and she isn't that big."

"Neither are you, Deb."

"Yes I am," she groans, squeezing her left thigh. "I can barely zip up these jeans."

"Girl, nobody wants a bone but a dog."

We are barely into the first month of school and Deb is already stressin' about her appearance. She's become completely obsessed with losing weight. Every day, while Juan and I are gettin' our grub on, Deb nibbles on soup and crackers or a salad. She used to eat a salad with olive oil until she found out olive oil has calories and switched to lemon juice. "What are you, about an eleven?" I ask.

"Ohmigod, no," she shrieks. "I wear a five."

"Deb, you're a size five and you think you're fat."

"My stomach is the real problem," she groans, trying to suck it in. Her pained expression and the tears that well up in her eyes let me know she's serious.

"Well, if you think a five's big, I won't even tell you what size I am."

"Tell me," she says, suddenly intrigued.

"It's not a five."

"An eleven," she leans in and whispers, as if embarrassed for me.

"A thirteen," I say, loud and proud.

"Are you okay?" she asks as if I just announced I had a deadly disease.

"I'm fine."

"Wow, Eboni. I had no idea you were that big. I'd be depressed if I wore a size thirteen. Don't you want to at least get down to like a single digit?"

"I never really thought about it. Back home my girls and I wore different sizes, but we didn't obsess about losing weight. We just rolled together and had fun."

"But you see the girls at school sportin' all the hot clothes."

"So do you. Why are you comparing yourself to them?"

"I'm not. I just want to look good, too."

"You do look good," I try to reassure her. "But you seem

a little obsessive. As my father told me, 'Every girl is a diamond; never forget how valuable you are.'"

"I'm not obsessed," she shoots back defensively, completely missing the last part of my statement. "I just don't want to be—" She pauses.

"What? Fat?"

"Well, yeah. But I didn't want to hurt your feelings."

"You didn't," I assure her. "I'm fat-a-bulous! I've never had a problem with my weight and neither have any of my boyfriends."

"I wish I had your confidence, Eboni. My mom and I usually diet together, but will you do it with me this time?" she begs. "Please."

"It sounds too crazy to me."

"It won't be that bad. We just have to cut out complex carbs and exercise seven days a week."

"Seven days a week!" I shriek. I don't even like the three days of gym I have to take.

"C'mon, girl."

"You do realize I work at McDonald's on weekends, right?"

"Willpower, E. You don't have to get skinny. Just accentuate your curves."

"I'll think about it."

The rest of the bus ride home Deb and I sit in silence. She may be thinking about getting into smaller jeans, but I'm wondering if this is what I have to do to fit in out here. In some ways, I have the same issues as Deb. I want to fit in, too. But why can't I do it as I am.

Dear God,

Is there something wrong with me? With the way I look? I always thought I looked great, but every day I see all of these girls running around in tube tops and miniskirts and, well, they look cute. I want to wear them, too, but I'm not sure short shorts look good on me. I'm in this new town. With these new kids, maybe I should try something new. I don't believe that You designed us to all look alike, but it would be nice to rock some of the latest trends— tastefully, of course.

Chapter 11

What do you think he meant?" I drill Robin as we study for an upcoming debate.

"Tell me what happened again."

"I passed him in the hall. He looked at me and spoke," I tell Robin of my close encounter with G.

"What did he say?"

"He said, 'What's up?' I turned around to see who he was talking to and he said, 'I'm talkin' to you, shorty. What's your name?' I was in shock, but managed to tell him my name. Then he asked if I was new. I told him I had just moved here from Baltimore. Then he said, 'Oh, B-More, huh? I could tell you weren't from around here,' and looked me over from head to toe. That's as far as the conversation got before his boys pulled him away. Then he simply said, 'Later, B-More.'"

"I think he meant that you don't look like you're from around here," Robin responds sarcastically.

"What exactly does that mean? Does it mean I look crazy? I look good? What?"

"No, Eboni. You don't look crazy. You may act crazy sometimes. Like now, when we've got to study."

"C'mon, Robin, this is serious."

"Look, I think you're putting *way* too much on it. Why do you even care what Gene Hicks thinks, anyway? He's just a dumb jock."

"Uh, maybe because he's the finest dumb jock on campus and out of the blue he notices me and says, 'I can tell you're not from around here.' That doesn't sound cool."

"Well, you aren't from around here," she reasons. "Ever stop to think that's why he noticed you? It's not a bad thing that you're not from L.A., or that you don't look like these skeletons running around on campus. You're always talking about how you and your girls in Baltimore are different from the girls in L.A. Maybe that's what he saw, the Baltimore Eboni. Not the crazy one I'm trying to study with, or the fun one who I think is cool."

"You're cool, too, Robin. That's why you're my girl."

"Sometimes I wish I wasn't from around here," she declares. "That's why I like you. You're real."

"Thanks."

"If you're that curious about what he meant, next time you see him, ask him."

"Maybe I will."

"You never know," she says. "He's everywhere on campus, just stop him and ask him. Now, can we get back to debate, please?"

"Sure. You need all the help you can get," I tease.

"Whatever." She laughs, rolling her eyes.

From: Michellettc@aol.com
To: Ebonieyesttc@aol.com
Subject: TTC Update

What up E,

Just reachin' out. Hadn't heard from you in a minute. Charisse and I cheered our first football game Friday and nearly froze our @sses off. Millwood lost, though. What's goin' on with you? Anybody catch your eye yet? I don't know if I told you the latest. Big Mike and I hooked up!!! NO WE DIDN'T DO IT YET! But girl, that boy can kiss! And his lips are so damn soft and juicy I could kiss him all day. I think I'm in love. We've been out twice and I'm seriously THINKIN' ABOUT GIVIN' HIM SOME. We came close a couple of times. He keeps asking me to do it, but I've managed to fight him off so far. But I don't know how much longer I'm going to be able to resist.

Okay, that's it for now. Hit me back with some Cali news soon. Until then, check out the picture attached of us!

M
TTC

I click download.

From: Ebonieyesttc@aol.com
To: Michellettc@aol.com
Subject: Cali Update

Girl, that picture is too cute with you fly girls smiling in your blue-and-gold Millwood cheerleading uniforms. I wish I was in it with you. It's still real warm here. It feels kind of crazy to be sportin' shorts in the fall. I can't believe you and Mike. I have my eye on this fine guy, Gene Hicks but they call him G. He plays on the football team. Of course, the body's bangin' and his smile is so damn sexy with perfectly white teeth, he could easily star in his own Colgate toothpaste commercial. But just like Vincent, everybody wants him. I don't know what it is about athletes. I just can't resist them, either. My girl Robin says I should just approach him next time and strike up a conversation. You know that's not my style. Besides, he's never by himself. We'll see what happens. I'm taking it real slow.

It's wild out here. I haven't met one girl who isn't a stick. The one time G and I spoke he said he could tell I wasn't from around here. But he didn't explain what that means.

Here, appearance is everything. Everybody looks like they belong in front of a camera, especially at Beacon Hills. What's even crazier is how much all of this is occupying my life. I bet that's what G was talkin' about when he said, "I can tell you aren't from around here." I'm sure he meant it's because I'm not a stick. So what I'm not a size three or even a five. Why does that have to make a difference? Corey says, "Find your spotlight and shine." *That's what I'm trying to do.* But everyone in Cali is trying to shine.

I've attached a photo of Deb and me on the first day of school.

Miss you,

E

Chapter 12

Debate is, without a doubt, my favorite class. Mr. Hinds makes it interesting and allows us to express our opinions freely. For our first debate, on the pros and cons of iPods, Robin was my partner. While she extolled the virtues of these new revolutionary devices, I took the counterpoint and cited cases of how iPod usage had caused pacemaker malfunctions and hearing loss. I also found reports of how mechanical glitches required consumers to replace them frequently and exposed how it was all a ploy by the manufacturer to keep people buying them. That debate got me an A.

The second one was on voter rights, and it proved to be more challenging, because I had to argue which presidential candidate was worthy of my vote. Though neither seemed to be, I managed to effectively argue why one outweighed the other. That one earned me a B.

But it is the third, on rap music, that is the most personal. I was all set to debate the con side until Mr. Hinds threw me a curve and asked that I take the pro. This time, my opponent is a skateboarder named Bryce Wellington, and I am determined to take him down.

"So, you ready, E?" Robin asks.

"Yep," I say, shuffling through my index cards.

"You remember what I told you, right?"

"Yeah. Hit him with a strong line to start. Make each point short and sweet, then nail him with an effective closing statement."

"Miss Imes, you're next," Mr. Hinds announces.

I take a deep breath and head for the podium. After composing myself, I begin. "Contrary to popular belief, there is a positive side to hip-hop. Today, hip-hop is *the* new rock 'n' roll: a global phenomenon. Young entrepreneurs that may not have otherwise been given opportunities to own companies have become successful millionaires because of it. Strong, positive voices have also emerged, such as Public Enemy, Talib Kweli, KRS-One, Jay-Z, and Queen Latifah, who have all voiced political and social concerns to our generation. When rap began more than twenty years ago in the Bronx, New York, people called it a fad and said it wouldn't last. They were wrong. Today, all of us, whether we live behind the gates of Bel-Air, or on the streets of South Central, listen to it on our iPods and have made hip-hop the most profitable music form in the world. Most important, though, it isn't just music. Hip-hop is a profitable, multibillion-dollar lifestyle. Thank you."

There's stunned silence until Mr. Hinds starts to clap. "Bravo, Miss Imes."

"Thank you, sir." I stroll back to my seat, head held high, and sit down.

"You rocked the hell out of that one, girlfriend," Robin whispers.

I can't wait to see how my opponent is going to handle it. "Thanks." I smile, feeling a great sense of accomplishment.

I glance at Bryce who's wearing a black T-shirt that says, IF THE MUSIC IS TOO LOUD, THEN YOU'RE TOO OLD. "Mr. Wellington, you're up next," Mr. Hinds announces. Bryce stumbles to the front, looking like he just rolled off his board, and proceeds to bore everyone until none of us, including Mr. Hinds, can take it any longer. "Uh, Mr. Wellington," Mr. Hinds cuts him off mid-sentence. "That's quite enough. Sit down."

"Class," he says, "I challenge you to take these debates seriously and arrive prepared like Miss Imes has done. Passion makes for great debates. Miss Imes was passionate. Her points were clear and concise. Like I told you on our first day, this is a popular elective. You're lucky to be here. Please act like you appreciate the fact that you are."

The bell rings and everyone jumps up. Clearly annoyed, Bryce passes without even acknowledging me. "Guess you pissed him off." Robin smirks.

"Oh well." I grin. "He'll get over it."

"Miss Imes, may I see you, please," Mr. Hinds says while gathering his newspapers.

"Yes, sir?"

"I'm very impressed by your grasp of the subject and your execution of it. In fact, you've impressed me with every single one of your debates. Whether pro or con, you always manage to pull it off effectively."

"Thank you, Mr. Hinds."

"Have you considered running for student council?"

"Me?"

"Yes. You've got quite a perspective. Elections are coming up soon."

"I hadn't really thought about it."

"Well, you should. Beacon Hills could definitely use your voice. Give it some thought. See you Friday."

"Yes, sir."

Dear God,

It felt good to get my points across and hear Mr. Hinds compliment me on how well I did. What I wasn't ready for was his suggestion that I run for student council. Finding my voice in debate is one thing. Running for student government is something totally different—and scary. How would I do it? What would I say? Would anyone even vote for an outsider like me?

Oh, and God, do you think G likes me?

O*kay, y'all,* I'm thinking about running for student council president," I announce to Deb, Juan, and Robin at lunch, on the front lawn.

"It's a lot of work," Deb warns, sipping a bottle of peach iced tea. "Meetings and stuff. You ready for all of that?"

"Sure she is," Robin chimes in supportively. "You should go for it. You'll be great."

"Mr. Hinds says they'll be gearing up for elections in a few weeks. So I still have some time to think about it."

"Well, if you decide to go for it, I'll help you," Robin promises.

"Thanks. What about you, Juanie? The Gay and Lesbian Club is gearing up, too."

"Ooh no, chile! I'm not a student government–type girl, too many rules. I don't do well with rules."

"But we could work to change things together around here."

"That's okay. I'd rather just dress the hell outta you."

"You'd do that for me?"

"Of course." He winks. "A diva's gotta look the part." Having Robin and Juan in my corner means a lot, especially for all the work it's gonna take to win.

"I'm down, too," Deb adds.

"Well, it looks like you've got your campaign committee," Robin says. "All you gotta do is say the word."

"I'll let you guys know what I decide, soon."

Later that night, I catch Mom in bed reading. "Hey."

"Hey, honey," she says, setting her book aside. "Climb in." I get in bed next to her and lay back for a heart-to-heart chat. "So, how was your day?"

"Good. Whatcha reading?"

"The new Barack Obama book. I'm really enjoying it."

"Guess what?"

"What?" she says, turning her attention to me.

"My debate teacher thinks I should run for student council."

"Really?" she says, excited. "Well, what do you think?"

"I'm thinking about it. Deb, Robin, and Juan offered to help if I do decide to."

"That's great."

"It's a lot of work, though, in addition to all my home-work and work at the restaurant."

"I'm sure you can handle it, honey."

"I just don't know if I can win. No one knows me here."

"Well, you've got to get out there and meet people. Let them know who you are and what you'll bring to the school," she suggests.

"That's just it. I don't know myself. You saw that school, Ma. Those kids have everything. They roll to school in Porsches and Range Rovers. What can I possibly offer them that they don't already have? I've gotta find a way to keep up."

"Let me tell you something," she says, laying down the book. "You aren't there to keep up with those kids."

"But how can I avoid it?"

"By not buying into it," she counters. "Eboni, you're at Beacon Hills to get a very good education. Do not get caught up in this foolishness about trying to keep up with those kids from a material, superficial angle."

"But, Mom," I say, intending to convince her that keeping up is crucial.

"But nothing," she interrupts. "Your father and I aren't in a position to help you live the high life. We have a new business to run, a mortgage to pay. Yvette is in college, and you still have to go. Money doesn't grow on trees. You got a phone and a television with cable *in your room*," she empha-sizes, "and you twisted your father's arm into getting you that Sidekick when all you really needed was a basic phone. I hope you don't start whining for more. Is that clear?" she says sternly.

"Yes, ma'am," I respond, realizing I'm not going to win this debate. "Well, I've still got homework to finish. I'll see you in the morning."

Mom looks at me thoughtfully. "Remember how I've always told you not to worry so much? Just do your best and the Man Upstairs will do the rest."

"Yes."

"I'm glad you're thinking of getting involved in student government, but I want you to find a way to do it without it costing us a lot of money, honey."

"I understand."

"Like Mimmie used to say, 'If you're gonna pray, then don't worry, and if you're gonna worry, then don't waste your time prayin'.' Now give me a kiss good-night."

I wrap my arms around her. "Thanks for the pep talk."

"You're welcome, baby."

* * *

From: Michellettc@aol.com
To: Ebonieyesttc@aol.com
Re: Cali Update

Hey E,

Sorry it's taken me a few days to hit you back. I've been goin' thru some things. The girls and I had to squash some craziness after this chicken head came at me about Mike. She tried to tell me he was her man and I needed to leave him alone. I told her he never mentioned her to me and that if she was his girlfriend, she needed to take our hanging out up with him. She wasn't hearin' me, though, and tried to swing on me, so you know me, I had to whip her. It was a big, crazy ordeal and I got suspended for a few days. My mom wasn't too happy about it, so I've been on lock-down. Things are cool now, though. What's going on in your world? Any updates on your boy, G?

M

From: Ebonieyesttc@aol.com
To: Michellettc@aol.com
Re: Cali Update

Hey Girlie,
Scared of you Laila Ali. Mike's got you fighting over him now. What kinda spell does he have on you? And are you sure he isn't playing both of y'all? Compared to all the madness you got goin' on, my life seems real boring. No updates on the G front. But I do need your opinion on something. I'm considering running for student council. What do you think? I need a campaign platform. I need money. Any suggestions?

E

Chapter 13

Okay, *that top right there* is calling my name," Deb coos, eyeing a salmon-colored satin halter in the window of Bebe. "I gotta try it on."

"Eboni, help me find an extra small," she says, rummaging through a pile of skimpy tops.

"You're kidding, right?"

"No," she gushes, picking one up and then striding toward a rack of dresses.

"Dang, girl. Slow down." She doesn't hear me, though. Instead, she's deep in the shopping zone.

"Do you need help?" a perky salesgirl in a tight-fitting top and capris inquires.

"Yes, do you have these in a—"

"The biggest is a medium." She cuts me off. "You look like a large."

You look like a Q-tip, I intend to scream, but it comes out of my mouth barely audible.

"What about this one?" I counter, holding up a pair of

faded, cropped jeans with ribbons around the belt loops.

"Let me see," she says, going through a nearby rack. "We didn't get many large sizes. The biggest is an eleven."

"I can wear that," I lie. I am determined to make the elevens work. I grab a couple of tops before heading for the dressing room.

"Are you in here, Deb?"

"Right here," she chirps, holding her hand up so I can see it.

"I'm next door."

When the clothes come off, I stand in front of the mirror for a minute and stare at my body. Though my tummy isn't as flat as a board and my waist isn't small, I like what I see. "Okay, Eboni, is this hot or what?" Deb squeals.

I open the door to check out her ensemble. "That's really cute. Turn around."

She does her best *America's Next Top Model* twirl. "What do you think?"

"Girl, Miss J would be proud of you," I joke, referring to my favorite judge on the show. That's when I suddenly see bones protruding through Deb's skin and notice that the jeans are swimming on her.

"This fits my curves in all the right places."

"Really?" I question.

"Yep."

"Where are they?"

"What's that supposed to mean?" she snaps.

"I was just kidding."

Deb doesn't say a word. She just goes back into her dressing room and slams the door. I slam mine, too, and attempt to remove the too-tight jeans that are cutting off my circulation. "You aren't mad at me, are you?" I ask as she gives me the silent treatment while paying for her purchases.

"No. But you always seem to have something negative to say."

"Well, sorry. I wasn't trying to be mean."

We exit Bebe and walk to the Guess store in silence. "Check out those earrings," Deb gushes. "Nina Ross had on the exact same pair on the cover of *Cosmo Girl*."

All I can think about is how sickly Nina Ross is and how much Deb seems to want to look just like her. All of a sudden, I can't stand to hear any more about the woes of the weight-challenged, especially now that Deb is becoming one of them. "All of this shopping is making me hungry," I announce. "Let's get something to eat."

"Let's hit Forever 21 first. It's right next to the food court," she whines.

"Fine." We head up the escalator as two fine guys, one with neat cornrows, a killer smile, and a T-shirt that reads TEENAGE MILLIONAIRE, are headed down. "Check out the millionaire," Deb whispers, forgetting all about our blowup.

"I'm checking," I reply. "Looks nice to me."

"Hey, thickums." He winks as we pass each other. "You make big beautiful," he flirts, reaching out to touch my hand.

"Hey." I blush, glad to see someone in this town appreciates my beauty.

"Did that boy just call you 'thickums'?" Deb snickers.

"At least he knows a real sistah when he sees one."

"Whatever," she sniffs. "I wasn't feelin' him or the braids, anyway."

"Hater," I tease before turning around for a second peek, surprised to see that he's looking back at me, too.

"That's just disrespectful," Deb spits as she heads into the store.

"I'll wait for you out here," I decide, not feeling her or anything in the window.

"You don't want to see if they've got anything cute?"

"Nah, I'm cool," I reply, frustrated by this unproductive day at the mall.

"Okay. I'll be quick."

As I check out the shoppers, "Mr. Teenage Millionaire" steps off the escalator. Panic is my first emotion, so I turn toward the store window and play it off like I'm checking out things. "Hey again," his smooth voice greets me.

I turn around and attempt to look surprised. "Hey."

"How you doin'?"

"I'm fine."

"You sure are," he flirts. "What's your name?"

"Eboni."

"Eboni, huh? I like that. I'm Darryl, but my peeps call me D-Nice," he offers, extending his hand.

"You work here?" I inquire, trying to strike up a conversation.

"Naw. My boy works for Puffy. He's doing a signing at Bloomingdale's for his new cologne. After we leave this bougie mall we're headin' over to the real spot, Fox Hills."

"What's that?"

"You never heard of the Fox Hills Mall?"

"No. I just moved here from Baltimore a few months ago."

"Oh, an East Coast honey, huh? I should've known. 'Cause they don't grow them like you out here."

"Tell me about it."

"Fox Hills Mall is in Culver City. It's *our* mall if you know what I mean. They got stuff to fit all them curves you got goin' on," he compliments.

"Oh, really?"

"Really," he continues to flatter.

"That sounds like where I need to be 'cause I'm not havin' any luck here."

"Yo, D . . . let's roll," his friend, who looks just like the rapper Nelly, shouts.

"Aiight." He gestures. "Hold up. Yo, look-a here, Miss Eboni. I gotta jet. You got a number?"

"Sure."

He pulls out a cell phone. "Okay, shoot."

Just as D-Nice and I are about to exchange digits, Deb comes barreling out of Forever 21 with a bag.

"All right, E, let's hit it. Not much luck here," she says, interrupting our mack session. "All I found was one measly baby tee and a couple of anklets. . . . Oh, I'm sorry." She stops in her tracks, clearly startled by the scene.

"Darryl, this is my friend Deb. Deb, Darryl."

"What's crackin'?"

"Hi," she says demurely.

Continuing where we left off, I give him my number. He punches the digits into his phone and closes it. "All right then. I'll holler at you later, thickums. Stay sweet."

"See ya." I smile, happy about our exchange.

"I can't believe that boy called you thickums and you're smiling."

"What's wrong with it? That's what I am."

"And you're cool with that?"

"Quite," I snap, trying to remain calm though I really want to go off. Instead, I change the subject. "So, what're you feelin' like, Panda Express or Sbarro?"

"Neither, really. Maybe I'll just grab some nonfat frozen yogurt."

"Nonfat yogurt is not a meal. It's a snack," I let her know straight-up. The last thing I want is to hear her talk stuff about my lunch selection. "Fine, get what you want. I'll get what I want and we can meet at a table."

"Okay," she says, looking around.

I make my way to Panda Express, but before I can order, Deb is right behind me. "Maybe I'll get Chinese, too," she says.

"I'll have the three combo with orange chicken, garlic shrimp, and beef with broccoli," I say to a round Asian woman.

"Rice or chow mein?" she asks.

"Half and half."

"You want egg roll for a dollar more?"

"Sure. Why not."

"That's gotta be about a thousand calories," Deb scolds, looking at my tray.

"Well, they're my thousand calories, not yours," I shoot back.

"Next." The lady looks to Deb.

"I'll take the steamed veggies and the eggplant with tofu, please."

"You want rice or chow mein?"

"Neither," she retorts.

"Figures," I utter under my breath, not surprised.

Sick of size-two salesgirls, squeezing into clothes that don't fit, and Deb's criticisms, I find a table and try to remain calm. "I can't believe you gave that guy your telephone number," Deb starts in the minute she sits down. "He could be crazy."

"You're crazy and I still hang out with you," I contend, spearing a chunk of orange chicken with my fork.

"Whatever, E." Deb chuckles. "I'm just saying, he seemed like he could be . . ." She trails off, trying to find the right word.

"What?"

"Ghetto," she says, popping a bean pod in her mouth.

"I didn't think so."

"And he seemed kinda pushy," she continues.

"Let me ask you a question," I say, dropping my fork.

"What?"

"Are you mad because he didn't try to talk to you?"

"Girl, puhleez," Deb responds flippantly. "I saw him checkin' me out when we were on the escalator, but he's not my type at all. I don't do braids."

"You didn't seem to have a problem with him before he started talking to me."

"Seriously, Eboni, I really wasn't feelin' him."

"And, clearly, he wasn't feelin' you either. That's why he came back to talk to me."

"Okay, thickums," Deb mocks. "I'm happy for you. Feel better?"

Her sarcastic tone pisses me off even more. "That's right. I am thick and I don't have to look like a toothpick to get attention."

"I don't look like a toothpick," she shoots back defensively.

"Girl, in the dressing room at Bebe, I could see your collarbone and ribs."

"Eboni, why do you have to be so dramatic? Of course you can see my collarbone. We all have them."

"Yeah, but we don't have them pokin' through our skin."

"I've been on a diet, remember?"

"Who can forget? It's all you talk about. How much have you lost, anyway?"

"Just ten," she says casually.

"Ten pounds already?"

"Why are you yelling? I look good whether you think so or not."

"You looked great ten pounds ago," I offer, but she isn't buying it. "Girls are supposed to have curves. Not look like boys."

She opens a packet, pops a few pills in her mouth, and chases it with a cup of lemon water. "Or pop diet pills."

"Vitamins," she snaps. "They're vitamins."

"Call 'em what you want, but they're not vitamins, Deb. There's no way you could lose that much weight that fast without some help."

"I've been exercising, too, thank you very much."

"Whatever," I say, exasperated by this taxing conversation. "Why do you want to look all sickly, anyway?"

"I don't," she says, trying to convince me. "I want to look leaner. Now that I'm losing weight my clothes fit better. Don't hate on me, Eboni, just because I found cute stuff in every store and you haven't."

"I'm not hatin', Deb. I even told you that you looked nice, but I thought you looked nice before this crazy-ass crash diet."

"Well, I didn't. And now I do."

"Well that's all that's important then." I give up. "Never mind being healthy as long as you're thin."

"You could stand to lose a few pounds, too. Look at that plate. That's way too much to be eating at one time."

"Listen, even if I did go on a diet I wouldn't kill myself like you're doing."

"I'm not killing myself," she shouts, causing an elderly couple to stare. "Look, Eboni. I'm sorry if I hurt your feelings. I wasn't trying to say that guys couldn't like you because you're big. I just want us both to look hot."

"I do, too. But I feel like you think the only way for that to happen is if we're both skinny and I just don't agree."

"Well, you saw for yourself how hard it is to find clothes that look good in bigger sizes. Every store we went into, nothing fit you."

Deb is so caught up in her brand-new body that she isn't hearing what I'm saying. "Then we'll just have to find stores that have cute stuff to fit me."

"Like where?"

"Are there any stores in this mall that carry bigger sizes?"

She looks at me like I'm speaking a foreign language. "If so, I don't know where it is. I've never been in one."

"Well, I heard they got tons of cute stuff in my size at the Fox Hills Mall. Will you go with me there?"

From: Ebonieyesttc@aol.com
To: Michellettc@aol.com
Re: Cali Update

Hey 'Chelle,
Check out this craziness. Today I went to the Beverly Center with Deb and we nearly came to blows in the middle of the food court. I don't know how things got so out of control, but since she's been on this crazy diet, 'ole girl just isn't rational. Things were cool as long as it was all about her. But, baby, the minute we saw these cute guys and one of them was checkin' me out instead of her, girlfriend couldn't handle it. And the day was a total waste of time for me because this mall doesn't have one plus-size store in it. When this guy hipped me to the mall where I could find stuff in my size that's fly, I asked her to go with me and she acted like she didn't want to be caught dead in Torrid or Ashley Stewart. She didn't even know what Torrid was.

I can't stand the fact that out here, it's all about what you've got on. How you look. And if you don't look a certain way, then you're not cool. I didn't have these issues in

B-More. And I don't want to have them here. But I'm not in B-More now. Girl, hit me back. I need to hear from you 'cause I ain't feelin' L.A. right now.

On a less frustrating note, what's up with you and Mike? Have things cooled down?

Love,

E

From: Michellettc@aol.com
To: Ebonieyesttc@aol.com
Re: Cali Update

Hey E,

Sounds like your new friend is a trip. Don't let it get you down, though. You've always found a way to shine. Hell no, you shouldn't lose weight. Unless you want to. Ask yourself this. What is it that you want to do that you haven't been able to do because you aren't a stick? If the answer is nothing, then do what you've always done. Do you! Continue to be the beautiful person that I've known since second grade.

Things with Mike and me are good again. We've been hangin' out a lot more. I guess he got that crazy girl straight because she hasn't been a problem anymore. Charisse and YoYo are doin' all right, too. They told me to tell you what's up.

M

Chapter 14

A *few days later,* after our Beverly Center blowup, Deb apologized and offered to go with me to Fox Hills. The minute we walked into Torrid, it didn't take long for me to find a fly two-piece jean suit and a pair of Apple Bottoms that fit like a glove. Paired with an off-the-shoulder black top, I am ready for my first high school homecoming.

The big game is only a few days away and the campus is buzzin' with excitement. The Panthers are six and two for the season and set to take on our crosstown rivals, Inglewood High, or "The Wood," as they are known.

"Any ideas who's performing at the homecoming dance?" I ask the crew while we're kickin' it in our usual lunch spot on the lawn.

"I heard maybe Matchbox Twenty," Juan chimes in, nibbling on a salad. Deb had convinced him to eat better and he, like me, is attempting to do so. I've decided to take Michelle's advice and be the best Eboni I can be, not go on that crazy diet with Deb. I don't see anything wrong with eating healthier, though. A compromise is to give myself one cheat day where I can eat anything I want. Every other day, I try to make healthy choices.

"I heard it may be Ashley Simpson or Green Day," Robin adds to the speculation.

"Somebody told me they heard on the low-low it may be Beyoncé and Jay-Z," I inform them of the rumors swirling around the campus.

"Ohmigod, clutch pearls," Juan squeals and nearly spills his entire tray. "Honey, if Miss B comes here y'all might have to restrain me. That girl is the most down diva there is. Have you seen her clothing line?" Before we could answer, he continues to babble on, "If I see her, I may have to beg her and her mama for a job."

"Homecoming would fall on the craziest week for me," I moan, opening a bottle of iced green tea, a tasty discovery since moving West.

"Tell me about it," Robin concurs, stabbing a chunk of meat from her Chinese chicken salad. "I haven't even started studying for the next debate yet."

"Mr. Hale sprung a science pop quiz on us *and* I've got an English report due."

"You'd think they'd chill with piling on the homework since they know it's party time," Juan groans. "All I care about right now is what I'm wearing and who's performing."

"Anybody seen Deb?" I inquire.

"I saw her earlier. She said she wasn't feeling well," Juan shares.

"I'll call her when I get home."

✳   ✳   ✳

Hey, Juan said you were sick."

"Yeah. My mom had to come pick me up."

"What happened?"

"I was in gym and felt light-headed. I tried to go over and get some water but before I could make it to the fountain, I passed out. The teacher got me to the nurse and she said I was dehydrated and needed to drink plenty of fluids. But I'm cool now. You ready?"

"Are you sure we should be walking today? Maybe you should take it easy."

"Girl, please. I'm fine. I'll come right over to get you."

Deb had persuaded me to walk with her three times a week as if walking home from school and gym class wasn't exercise enough. "How much have you lost?" she asks immediately when I open the door. I step out and we head for a nearby trail.

"I don't know. I haven't gotten on the scale lately." Though I'd decided to eat healthier, changing the person I am to fit in has never been cool.

"What about you?" I ask, genuinely concerned.

"I think I lost a couple more pounds," she announces proudly.

"Deb, please be careful."

"I know. I can't believe it. This diet is da bomb. It's like the weight just melts right off."

"Are you sure it's safe?"

"I feel fine and I look okay, right?"

"It's not safe if you're passing out. Besides, you looked okay before you decided to become a stick."

"Thanks, E, but you don't have to try to be nice."

"I'm not. It's true."

Walking with Deb is my way of being supportive. Though I dread it some days, when we really get going, I enjoy our hikes. It's a way to forget about the pressures of Beacon Hills.

"Let's go this way," she suggests, leading the way in red-and-white nylon shorts with a matching sleeveless Nike Goddess T-shirt. "I found this other trail I want to try."

"Okay, but no more hills," I protest, worn out from the first two we'd tackled.

"I got something I want you to try with me."

"What?"

She pulls a brown package from her sock.

"What's that?"

"Cloves," she informs me, pulling one from the colorful package.

"What are cloves?"

"They're these funky little cigarettes Juan gave me."

"You got me out here exercising, and you wanna stop for a smoke break? What kind of sense does that make?"

"What?" she says defensively. "It's not like we're gonna turn into pack-a-day smokers. We're just trying something cool and new, that's all."

"Okay, fine, I'm down. But make sure nobody's coming."

"This looks like a cool spot," she says, kneeling down in a hidden stretch of hill. My heart starts to race as I put the cigarette to my lips. "My mother would kill me if she saw us right now," I tell her, trying to steady my hand to strike the match.

"Girl, your mama doesn't have to know everything."

"Trust me. Your mother ain't like mine. If we accidentally set this hill on fire, she'll set my butt on fire."

"We won't." She laughs as I struggle to get the thin brown cigarette lit.

"I'll do it." She grabs the matches, lights her cigarette like a pro, then leans over and lights mine and tosses the match.

"Make sure it's out good."

"Calm down, Miss Scary." Deb stomps the match out with her red-and-white sneaker. "There. Feel better?"

"Yes." I sigh, inhaling deeply.

"Ooh, they're sweet," she says, licking her lips as we both get our puff on. "And they smell good, too. Juan was right. These are nice and light. I like them. They give me a buzz."

I take another puff and gaze out over the skyline in deep thought, feeling slightly lightheaded. If anyone had told me that my new crew would've been a gay Latin boy who dresses better than me, a laid-back Jewish girl, and a black girl with white parents, I never would've believed it. I'd never had any close friends of other races, but in just a few short months, I'd grown to rely on these three.

"Deb," I break the silence.

"Yeah," she answers, turning to me.

"Can I ask you a question?"

"Sure."

"Are you adopted?"

The minute I finish the sentence and see the pained expression on her face, I regret asking, but it had been on my mind since our first meeting and I finally felt cool about asking her. "Sort of," she says calmly. "When I was five, my father killed my mother."

"Oh my God, Deb. If it's too difficult, we don't have to go there."

"It's okay. One night, my parents got into a fight and my father pushed her and she fell back on the sofa," she says slowly. "She hit her head on the edge of the coffee table."

"Did you see it happen?"

"I watched from the stairs like I did whenever their voices got loud."

"How old were you?"

"Five."

"Wow." I sigh. "I'm sorry, girl. That's horrible."

"It was an accident, though, because right after she fell, my father rushed to call 911. But by the time they got her to the hospital, she'd had a brain seizure. The police came to the hospital and charged my father with manslaughter. The Goldsteins took on his case, but they couldn't get him off," she continues, staring out over the city. "He was sent to prison and I haven't seen him since."

"That's tough."

"After the trial, they adopted me."

"Do you ever think about your father?"

"Sometimes," she offers thoughtfully. "I think about both of my parents and what my life would've been like if my mom hadn't died. What my father looks like now. Where he is. How he's doing. Whether he got remarried, if he had any more kids." She sighs. "Sometimes I even wonder if he thinks about me."

"Have you thought about asking the Goldsteins to help you find him?"

"Yeah, but they've done so much for me. I don't want them to think that I'm not grateful and that I want to find him and leave them."

"They might not think that."

"I don't know if I'm ready to go there yet. Maybe one day," she says, taking one last puff of her clove.

"I hear you. You know if the day comes and you decide that you want to find him, I got your back, right?"

"Thanks, E. That's why I love you. You don't judge me. You just accept me with all my craziness." She smiles. "I'm so glad you moved to L.A. and into my life."

I am genuinely touched by Deb's words. Where she is weak, I am strong, and vice versa. "Me too," I hear myself say, feeling a little buzzed. "I'm glad, too."

"Here."

"What's this?"

"Dentyne Ice. You can't smell like smoke. Your mother'll kill you." She smirks.

"Good lookin' out, homie." I grin, popping a piece in my mouth. "She'll kill you, too, you know."

"Oh, I know. Your mama don't play."

Dear God,
Thanks for this day. I want to pray for Deb. I had no

idea that she had been through so much in her life. Now I understand her a little bit better. She's hurting. That's probably why she's on this constant search for acceptance, but diet pills and smoking won't get her there. I just pray that she will realize how beautiful she already is and love herself enough to be happy.

Chapter 15

When *we finally get* to the bleachers for the game, everyone is in a party mood. The band is playing. The drill team is getting the stands up and the coed cheerleading squad made up of four male cheerleaders and four females are doing their high-flying routine. "Do you see him?" I ask as we find seats in the crowded stands.

"Who?" Deb smirks.

"You know who."

By now it's no secret that I have a mad crush on G. Since I can't be with him for real, talking about him is all that keeps me going.

"No, we don't see your baby's daddy," Juan interjects. "He's probably down there ridin' pine."

"Yeah, right." I laugh, checking out all the black and orange jerseys on the field to see if I could spot G's number five. It's an important game because Inglewood's quarterback, Phil Freeman, has talked stuff the entire week leading up to the game and it has gotten back to G that Freeman plans to squash him into the ground. It's also Freeman's senior year and he's determined that the Bandits be undefeated. "My man doesn't ride pine."

"Oh, so he's your man now," Deb teases.

"That's right."

"Does he know it?" Robin asks, getting in on the act. "'Cause, if not, I'd be more than happy to tell him for you."

"You mean does Maya know?" Deb jokes.

I shoot them both a look. "I don't need either of you to help me, thank you very much. He'll know soon enough."

"Really?" Deb pries. "When?"

"Soon," I reiterate, wondering just how to pull it off. "Don't worry about it."

"Girl, I ain't mad at ya about that one," Juan says. "He is a fine piece of work."

"Step off, boy."

"I understand you're afraid you might come up short. I have that effect on men," Juan hisses playfully.

"Okay you two, cut it out, there's plenty of cuties for all of us," Robin jumps in.

"You got that right," Deb says, eyeing a player from the opposing bench. "And we can start by checkin' out fine ass number twenty-three on Inglewood's bench."

We all stand up to see who Deb is talking about. "Second from the end." She points. "Is he fine or what?"

I notice a fair-skinned, curly-haired boy. "Girl, please. He ain't got nuthin' on G," I say as our band attempts to pump up the crowd. "If they play that tired fight song one more time, I'm gonna fight them."

"And I'm gonna join you."

By the end of the second quarter, Inglewood is up twenty-one to ten. "This is beyond humiliating," Robin says. "Whose bright idea was it to play the best school in the division for homecoming?"

"Two-four-six-eight, the Panthers are gonna annihilate," our pathetic squad, which includes Maya, chants, trying to get the crowd into it. "Someone oughta annihilate them for those tired routines." Deb laughs. "Apparently rhythm isn't a requirement."

"Or style," Juan groans. "Those skirts are a hot mess and what's with the knee socks. They should've consulted a fashionista. And those boys . . ." he continues, referring to the line of male cheerleaders.

"Still a little heated that you didn't make the squad," Deb rubs it in.

"Heck, nah. They did me a favor. I wouldn't be caught dead with those tired hags. Check out those sistahs over there." He snaps in the direction of the Inglewood squad. "I'd work it right alongside those divas in a heartbeat. Just watch them, they get down."

We all look over at the Bandit squad—two black, two white, and two Latinas—who're working it like crazy. "Clearly, you've gotta be able to cheer AND do all the latest dance moves," Robin observes.

"Now that's how you shake it." Juan jumps up and down. "All of them got it goin' on." We continue to marvel at the rival bench as their band's drum section starts banging a familiar tune and the entire Inglewood stand starts to party. "Yo, is that 50 Cent they're playin'?" I ask, impressed.

"Yep," Deb confirms.

"Okay, now that's the shiznit right there."

Juan continues to shake his booty as Inglewood's band goes from the 50 Cent joint into a Ludacris jam that sends the stands into another frantic scene. "Ooh, heeeyyy, that's my jam, too." Juan moves, jumping up to party again. "I may need to transfer next year."

"Well, E, I know what one of your campaign promises could be if you decide to run," Robin says, looking down on the field.

"What?"

"Some better moves and some sistahs in cheerleading uniforms," Juan stops dancing long enough to add. "'Cause, honey, our folks need to sit it down with those tired moves."

"There's one," I say, referring to Maya, the lone black girl in the line.

"She's just as tired as the rest of them," Juan observes.

With two minutes left in the fourth quarter, Inglewood had scored again, making the score twenty-eight to ten. I notice G remove his helmet in frustration as the coach talks to him. Then I notice him check out the stands and make eye contact with Maya. She blows him a kiss. He smiles, then sits down on the bench and drops his head in his hands. "Well, this game is a wrap," Deb predicts. "Freeman just scored another touchdown. We might as well head over to the swim gym and get a seat for the show."

* * *

kay, I know this isn't it," I say, entering the gym to find a few balloons next to a deejay booth. "Where are the decorations?"

"Where's the band?" Robin asks.

"Forget that. Where's the food?" Juan looks around.

Not only was there no band scheduled and no food, but the deejay was whack and everybody was just standing around bummed by our devastating loss to Inglewood. When the Panther players trickle in, G looks down-in-the-dumps. I decide to position myself in a spot where he has to pass me. When he does, I attempt to cheer him up. "Good game, G," I say as he approaches. Right after it comes from my lips I want to kick myself.

"Thanks, B-More," he says, dejected. "But in case you hadn't noticed, they beat us like we stole something."

"You'll get 'em next year."

"Right. Next year."

"I was just wondering," I continue, attempting to change the subject. Before I can finish my sentence, though, two of his teammates approach. "Yo G, ain't nuthin' poppin' up in here, we're 'bout to roll over to this other spot. You comin'?"

"Yeah," he says. "Hold up." They wait as he looks back at me. "You were sayin' something?"

"Uh . . . oh, nothing," I stutter. "Go ahead. We can talk later."

"Bet," he says, looking around the gym one last time. "Let's roll. I need somethin' to get me out of this funk."

"Or someone." His boy laughs.

"Even better." They high-five and that's when I overhear one of the guys in the group say, "Yo, man. Who's the fat honey?"

"A fan. You know how it is."

"Right," his boy says. "It sho' must be nice to be you, G."

All I can do after that dis is sit down in the stands and try to hold it together. This day had gone from bad to worse, and this tired dance was the icing on the cake. At this very moment, I wish I could close my eyes and be back in Baltimore and at Millwood with my girls. It didn't help that the deejay was spinnin' the same tired three songs over and over again. I couldn't take much more of this dud of a party, this crazy school, or this wacky city.

"Hey," Robin says, finding me sitting alone in the stands. "I saw you talking to G. How'd it go?"

"Horrible," I tell her. "One of his boys called me a fat honey and he called me a fan."

"He actually said that to your face?"

"No, I heard him say it as they were walking off."

"Girl, later for him and his jerky friends. They're not worth your time. Let's go. This dance is beyond tragic."

"I'm ready," I tell her, wiping my eyes so she can't see I'm on the verge of tears. "Where're Juan and Deb?"

"Trying to dance to this crazy music."

"Are we leaving them?"

"Heck, yeah. I'm done."

As Robin and I head for the door, I spot G's silver Honda parked across the street from campus and notice

Maya, still in her cheerleading uniform, with G's letter-man jacket wrapped around her, with her head stuck in his window. After a few minutes, she runs over to a yellow Volks-wagen Bug convertible driven by one of the Sticks, jumps in the passenger seat, and they take off. G is right behind them, followed by his boy in a black Mustang. My heart just aches. When I get home, it's time to have a chat with the Man Upstairs.

> *Dear God,*
> *All I really want to do right now is cry, because after that scene in the gym, it's clear I don't have a shot with G. Who am I kidding? I probably never did. I'm just some little fat freshman to him. I guess he's right. I am a fan, but he didn't have to say it in front of his boys. It was so embarrassing, especially when they laughed. Then to see Maya in his car and wearing his letterman jacket was too much. I don't know why I'm feelin' him like I am. I don't really even know him. And it's obvious that even though he spoke to me, he's not interested in getting to know me. The only thing I can do now is ask You to take my feelings for G Hicks away.*

I lie down in the bed, put on my headphones, and scroll to the T-Mac section of songs on my iPod and press play on his hit "Blaze." When he croons about how you've got to let your feelings burn in order to get over someone, I finally understand the true meaning of his song.

From: Michellettc@aol.com
To: Ebonieyesttc@aol.com
Re: Cali Update

Hey E,

How was your homecoming? Ours was off the hook. We shut Emerson High down. Girl, they didn't score at all. You should've seen Mike on the field. He scored two of Millwood's four touchdowns. I was so proud of my baby. The dance was the bomb, too. Deejay Melody threw down. After the dance, we went back to Mike's house. While everyone was gettin' their party on, we went up to his room and came close to doin' it, but I got nervous and slowed things down. I don't know if I'm gonna be able to hold out much longer, though, because I really want to do it. I just didn't want to do it with so many people around. I'm sure Beacon Hills did it big for homecoming! Can't wait to hear all about it.

Love,
'Chelle

From: Ebonieyesttc@aol.com
To: Michellettc@aol.com
Re: Cali Update

Hey Girl,

Wow. Sounds like you had a great weekend on the field and off. Our homecoming was beyond tired. I had the most embarrassing encounter with G. You know I've never been good at making the first move, and when I tried, it ended up backfiring and I got my face cracked—not cool. Call me old-fashioned, but if a guy is feelin' me, he's gonna have to make the first move. After that scene, I'm cool on G Hicks.

Love,

E

Dear God,

Maybe it's good G isn't pushin' up on me because I probably would've seriously considered letting him be my first, even though he proved tonight he doesn't deserve it. I can't change the fact that I'm a size thirteen black girl with body. I like my curves even if Gene Hicks can't appreciate them.

Chapter 16

Our last encounter has left me less than eager to see or even talk to G. But there is no avoiding him. He is "the man" on campus and that means he is everywhere. It's hard to get a read on him. One minute he's flirty and acts like he's feelin' me, the next minute he barely speaks. It is also difficult trying to figure out his crazy relationship with Maya. They aren't officially boyfriend and girlfriend, but there is definitely a connection of some kind. Instead of obsessing, I decide to let the chips fall where they may and enjoy my first sushi lunch.

"You cannot live in California, Eboni, and not have tried California rolls," Juan scolds.

"And edamame," Deb adds.

"Eda what?"

"Edamame. It's soy beans," Robin schools me. "They're good for you."

"And you've got to eat it all with chopsticks, except the edamame, of course. Here's how you do it," Robin says, removing a pair of chopsticks from a paper sleeve, pulling them apart, and rubbing them together.

"Okay, y'all, I've given it a lot of thought and I'm going for it," I announce.

"Goin' for what?" Juan asks, grabbing a colorful roll.

"Student council president."

Juan pats me on the back. "Do it, girlfriend."

"Robin, will you still be my campaign manager?"

"Definitely," she says without hesitation.

"Cool. Deb, will you co-manage?"

"Of course. Whatever you need me to do. I've got you, girl," she agrees, popping a soybean in her mouth.

"I'll be your image consultant. You're gonna need somebody to create your winning ensembles," Juan insists.

"Boy, I'm gonna need you to do more than that."

"Yes, dahlin', I understand, but your look is crucial to a victory. So, I'll start there. Everything else is secondary."

"If you say so."

"Oh, I say so."

The fact that the crew had my back was the confirmation I needed to proceed. Though I wasn't quite sure what my campaign platform would be, there were a few areas where I knew I could make a difference, like revving up our tired homecoming. "Okay. So, what should we tackle first?"

"A California roll," Deb instructs. "It's rice-wrapped seaweed with imitation crab, carrots, avocado, and cucumber."

"No, I'm talking about for the campaign," I say, grabbing a roll and dipping it in soy sauce. "Hey, that's pretty good."

"Well," Robin starts. "You could start with things you'd

like to change. It's also important for people to know what you stand for."

"Great idea," I say, writing it down.

"Oh, and you need a flyer with a photo wearing something hot," Juan adds.

"We also need some good giveaways for the campaign party," Deb suggests.

"Campaign party?"

"Yes," Robin insists. "It's a must."

"Where?"

"Don't know yet. We'll figure it out. Make sure you pick up the entry form, fill it out, and turn it in so it's official," Robin adds. "Then we can start planning how to get you elected."

"Got it."

"Okay, enough about the campaign," Deb says. "Let's eat some sushi."

All of these new taste sensations are overwhelming and surprisingly good until I notice Robin's puzzling selection. "Okay, what is that?" I ask, eyeing a small piece of fish resting on rice.

"Barbecued freshwater eel. It's so good. Try a piece."

"Oh, you're buggin'." I turn my nose up at the thought. "I don't do eel."

"Have you ever tried it?"

"No."

"Well, then, how do you know you don't like it?" Robin reasons.

"Because I don't even like the way it looks."

"Just try one piece and if you still think it's nasty, you don't have to eat any more."

"Fine." I pick up the eel, close my eyes, and stuff it in my mouth.

"Well?"

"It's not as bad as I thought, but I'm still not feelin' it," I say, grabbing a glass of water nearby to chase away the taste.

"Okay, well, try one of these," Juan says of a roll with orange-colored relish on top. "It's shrimp tempura roll. You might like this one. The shrimp is cooked."

I attempt to pick the roll up with my chopsticks and plop it in my mouth. "Okay, those are off the chain," I say, going for another one. "So far those are my favorite."

"I knew you'd like them." Juan winks. "They're my favorite, too."

"Here's an invite to the hottest birthday party of the year and it's goin' down at Maya's mansion. Saturday. Eight o'clock," one of the Sticks announces as she hands a group of skateboarders sitting at the table next to ours frilly invitations.

"Rad," a scruffy boy in a GIRLS GONE WILD FILM CREW T-shirt says, accepting the invite. "Maya's a total babe."

"Dude, I didn't even think she knew us," a tall one raves. "This is so cool."

"So Maya's having a big birthday party, huh. Did you get an invite?"

Robin tries to play off the question. "Robin," I reiterate. "Did Maya invite you to her party?"

"Yeah," she replies sheepishly. "I got one in second period."

"Sellout."

"What? We went to middle school together. It's gonna be a hot party."

"Whatever."

Maya's party was the last thing on my mind, especially since I wasn't in her inner circle of friends. "I thought of a slogan," I share, deciding to change the subject.

"What is it?"

"It's Time for a Change."

"I like it," Robin says. "Now all we have to do is define exactly what that means."

"I know. I'm still working on that part."

"It'll come to you."

From: Ebonieyesttc@aol.com
To: Michellettc@aol.com
Subject: The Election

Hey 'Chelle,

Well, it's official. I'm running for student council president. Juan, Deb, and Robin are my campaign committee. So far, we've come up with a campaign poster. Juan insisted on styling me. Deb did my makeup and Robin designed the posters. They came out so great, I almost didn't recognize myself. We strategically placed them all over campus so students can put a name with my face. At first, I wasn't sure about seeing myself around school that much, but the crew insisted. I took your advice and made sure to put a sign by the gym so G can see what he's missing. (Good lookin' out on that move.) This one boy passed while I was doing it and did a double take, then winked at me. I thought that was cute. People are starting to know Eboni Imes, which is all a part of our strategy. So far, I've come up with ideas for better food in the cafeteria, a more liberal tryout policy for drill team and cheerleading, and a better homecoming. I'm still trying to think of something bigger to really hit 'em with. It hasn't come to me yet, though.

Trying to run an election, focus on school, and work at the restaurant leaves me little time for anything else. Most days, I'm too tired, but I'm in it to win it, so I have to stay on point. I still gotta also try to figure out how to get the funds to throw a campaign party. If you have any suggestions, please let me know. I can use all the help I can get.

How's B-More? What are y'all up to? Miss you! Tell the girls I said "Hey."

M

Chapter 17

I don't know if I want to go," I tell Deb on the way home from school.

"Why not? It's gonna be fun."

"Because, you saw the way it went down. She didn't want to invite us. She damn near broke her arm handing us the invitations."

While Juan, Deb, and I were talking to a couple of girls from gym, one of the Sticks walked over and handed invitations to the girls we were talking to and also to Juan. When she got to Deb and me, she hesitated for a minute then looked at us like she felt sorry for us and reluctantly handed us invites, too.

"C'mon, Eboni. It'll be fun. Besides, I don't think Maya's girl would've given us invites if she thought Maya would trip. You know how they can be," Deb reasons.

"Exactly. They're bougie and stuck-up."

"Let's just go and have a good time."

"Fine," I concede, half-curious about Maya and how she lives. "Let's do it."

❋ ❋ ❋

Okay, *girls.* I can't drive and look at street signs, too,"
Mom says as she creeps along Sunset Boulevard on the way
to Maya's soiree, my first official big L.A. bash.

"I think the next one is Weatherly," I say, checking out
both sides of the wide street. "Getting lost wouldn't have
been an issue if we'd have gotten the minivan with the navi-
gation system."

"You're right about that." She chuckles. "But you know
your father. He thinks getting lost will help us learn our way
around."

"Yeah, well, right now it's making us miss the hottest
party of the year."

"Right here," Deb screams, scaring Mom and me as we
roll past the street. "Sorry," she says, seeing the terror on
our faces. "I just didn't want us to miss it."

Mom turns onto the street and I'm immediately awe-
struck. "Wow. These places are huge," I say, checkin' out
the mansions as we pass. "That one looks just like the house
on that show, *Fresh Prince of Bel-Air,*" I joke as we pass a huge
white Mediterranean-style home that sits behind a gate with
the letter P engraved in the middle.

"The P must stand for P-A-I-D," Deb jokes.

"Right."

"I think this is it," Mom says, stopping in front of a beautiful house with huge palm trees and a circular driveway
lined with expensive cars. "Okay, girls, Linda will be here at
eleven to pick you up."

Deb nudges me. "But, Mom. The party's not over until one."

"Well, you don't want to be the last ones to leave," she stresses. "And your curfew is eleven, Eboni. So do I need to come back and pick you up?"

"No, Mrs. Imes. Eleven is fine," Deb chimes in.

"Great. Glad we understand each other. Now you ladies have fun."

"Yes, ma'am," I groan, sliding the van door closed.

"Sorry, girl," I say, defeated. "She don't play that let's-negotiate stuff. If I make her too mad, she'll make both of us get our butts back in the car and drive us back home."

"I understand," Deb says. "Okay, how do I look?" she asks, posing.

"That top is bangin'. Red really looks good on you."

"Thanks."

"What about me?"

"E, you know you always look fly."

"It isn't easy, but somebody's gotta do it. Ready?"

"Ready." She wiggles, shaking off nervous energy.

We pass a statue of a naked woman holding a pot with water flowing from it. In the driveway sits a candy apple–red Ferrari, a Bentley like the one I saw in a Puffy video, and a Mercedes convertible. "This is my favorite car," I say, running my hand along the baby-blue Benz.

"I know. It's beautiful."

As we near a back gate, the gravelly voice of Busta Rhymes bellows.

"Well, the music's bangin'. That's a good sign," I say, eager to check out the festivities.

When we enter Maya's backyard, I'm not quite ready for the scene. It looks like the entire school is here. In one corner, three surfer dudes are flying down a slide and flipping into a huge swimming pool. A few feet away, are the jocks—including G, who looks fine in a pair of long shorts, Air Force Ones, and a wife-beater tank. He is shooting hoops with his boys, Jordan Adams and Matt Smith. I also notice a group of bikini-clad girls cheering them on from the sidelines. Not far away is another clique, dancin'. "Can you believe this place?" Deb whispers. "It's incredible."

"It's off the chain all right." I look around, noticing three buffet stations: one with hot dogs and burgers, another with freshly made pizzas, and a third with made-to-order sushi prepared by a sushi chef.

"Is that a bar?"

"A very well-stocked bar." Juan stumbles over to us with a glass in hand. "What took you so long?"

"We got lost," I confess.

"How long have you been here, Juanie?" Deb asks.

"Long enough to have three wonderful cocktails."

"And get drunk as a skunk," I add.

"I prefer to call it 'nicely buzzed.'"

"Well, show me the way," Deb coos. "I wanna get nicely buzzed, too."

"Follow me, *mamacitas*. The bartender and I are great friends."

We get into a long line for drinks. "What do you recommend?" Deb asks.

"The Maya-tini," Juan informs us.

"What'll it be, ladies?" an Ashton Kutcher look-alike asks, placing two napkins with Maya's initials down on the bar in front of us.

"I'll have another Mayatini." Juan winks.

"Make mine a Jack and Coke," Deb orders with confidence.

"Dang, girl. My father doesn't even drink that stuff."

"He doesn't know what he's missin'."

"And you?" He turns to me.

"I'll just have a glass of white wine."

"Coming right up."

"Aren't you sophisticated," Juan teases in a drunken stupor.

"Whatever, boy," I respond.

As Deb, Juan, and I chat, Maya suddenly appears, decked out in a red bikini with a matching floral sarong that sits just below a tattoo of an angel spreading its wings along the small of her back. The Sticks surround her, wearing matching white bikinis. Luckily, it is an unusually warm day. "All right, party people, let's hear it for the birthday girl who is making her grand and beautiful entrance. You're lookin' quite delicious in that red-hot bikini. You get applause for that," the deejay crows as Maya flashes a smile and eats up the compliment.

The guys hoot and holler as the girls look on and applaud. "Magnificent Maya, this one's for you," the deejay says as he spins "It's Your Birthday" by rapper 50 Cent and the entire party erupts in wild excitement. Maya wiggles to the music as the Sticks dance alongside her.

"Yo B-More, what's poppin'?" I hear a familiar voice say. I turn to see G standing beside me with a hot dog in hand. "So, you enjoyin' the festivities?"

"I just got here, but it seems cool," I say, trying to remain calm and detached after our homecoming encounter. But seeing him, I seem to be overcome by a sudden heat.

"So, did you bring your swimsuit?" he inquires, shoving half of the hot dog in his mouth. Even with mustard on his face, he's still fine.

"Maybe."

"Just askin' 'cause from the looks of things baby got cakes."

"I didn't think you liked cakes."

"I like it all," he says, checking out a trio of girls that pass.

As much as I didn't want to like him, I felt myself slipping back into the G zone. "Well, if you want—" he starts to say before we're interrupted, which seems to be a recurring theme for us.

"Hey, G," the scantily clad birthday girl purrs. "There you are."

"Yes." He smiles. "Here I am."

"Hi Maya. Thanks for the invite." What I really want to say is, *Get the hell out of here and leave us alone.*

"Sure," she utters, never taking her eyes off G. "We were about to hang out in the house for a bit. You down?"

"Hell, yeah." He grins wickedly.

"Round up your boys and meet us in the Red Room."

"Cool," he says, mesmerized, as Maya sashays away. "See you B-More." He winks.

"Yeah, see ya," I mumble to myself as the boy of my dreams walks away with the girl of my nightmares.

I decide to check out the rest of this palatial pad. The house is phat—from the Olympic-size swimming pool that makes ours look like a Jacuzzi to the tennis courts, where I notice Robin playing a game. "Robin," I scream over the music, hoping she can hear me. "Hey." She waves between lobs. After a long rally, she joins me. "So, you finally got here, huh?" Robin says, wiping her face with a towel.

"We got lost. Okay, this house is ridiculous," I say, looking around at the chaos that is Maya Williams's party.

"Yeah, it is."

"What do her parents do?"

"Her mother is the actress May Montgomery from the soap *The Young and the Restless*."

"Really?"

"Yeah. And her dad is a big-time music producer. He runs Big Ballin', that hip-hop record label."

"Must be nice. No wonder everybody's jockin' her."

"Yeah. She's definitely a BAP."

"What's a BAP?"

"You've heard of a Jewish American Princess? Well, she's a Black American Princess."

"Wow," is all I can say. "So they really do exist."

"Wanna play a game? I brought an extra racket."

"Nah. I think I'm gonna go check out the buffet. Try to line up a few votes."

"Good idea. See you in a minute," she says, heading back to the court.

"G'head, girl. Get your Serena Williams on," I tease, getting up to leave. "Oh, hey, have you seen Deb?"

"I saw her go into the house a few minutes ago. Probably to the bathroom."

"She's actin' like a wild woman with all this free liquor. I better check on her."

"You want me to come with you?"

"Please."

"Sure."

We set off in search of our girl. "I think this is the way," Robin says.

I open a sliding glass door to the inner sanctum of the high-powered Williams family. The interior—a sunken all-white living room with Italian marble floors, expensive art, ornate furnishings, and tons of framed photos of Maya and her famous mother and father—is just as fly as the outside. "Where do you think the bathroom is?"

"Who knows?" Robin shrugs as we tiptoe through the foyer. "This place is bigger than my entire apartment complex."

We walk along a hallway, pass a library, and suddenly hear laughter. "You hear that?"

"Yeah. Sounds like it's coming from that room at the end of the hall." We approach and peek through a cracked door to a room complete with a popcorn machine, plush seats, and a home theater.

"Can you see what's going on?" Robin whispers.

"It's hard to make out faces, but I can see G and his boys

and Maya and the Sticks," I inform her. "It looks like they're smoking something."

"What?"

"I don't know. Some crazy-looking hose."

Matt, one of G's teammates, takes a hit and passes the pipe to Maya, who inhales deeply. She passes the pipe to one of her girlfriends and then scoots close to Matt. They kiss and a puff of smoke passes from her mouth into his. He inhales deeply, then falls on top of her and they kiss passionately. The Sticks do the same thing and then kiss each other. G's and his boy Jordan's eyes get big as they sit back and watch the scene unfold. "Wow," I squeal to Robin. "This is bananas."

"What is it, Eboni? Let me see."

I step aside so Robin can take a peek for herself. "Oh," she says. "They're hitting a hookah."

"What the heck is a hookah?"

"It's a water pipe. Sometimes they fill 'em with molasses or dried fruit-flavored tobacco. It originated in the Middle East somewhere. When you smoke from it, you get a buzz."

"Let me look again."

As Robin and I watch the scene unfold, we suddenly hear a voice—and witness a sight—neither of us expected. "How'd you like that?" Deb pops up from behind a chair and asks G's boy Paul.

"That shit was hot," he replies with an expression of sheer bliss. "Now, do my boy." Everyone laughs as Deb happily moves from Paul to Matt and begins to unzip his pants. Robin and I are so stunned we can't move.

"Robin, please tell me that's not our girl in there."

"It is." She shakes her head in despair. "What are we gonna do?"

"We've got to get her outta there."

"I know, but how?"

"We're just gonna have to bust in."

"I'm right behind you," she says nervously.

"Okay, on three." I stand and get ready. "One . . . two . . . three."

"Deb," I scream, barging in and almost tripping over a pillow in the process. "What the hell are you doing?" The entire room freezes.

"Eboni!" Deb shrieks, pulling her top up. "What're you doin' in here?"

"What are *you* doin' in here?" I counter. "Are you out of your mind?"

"No."

"Do you wanna be down so bad that you're handing out blow jobs to random guys?"

"We were just havin' fun," she tries to convince me.

"Excuse you," Maya protests. "Why are you in my house?"

"We're here to get our friend," I say. "Right, Robin?"

"Right." She backs me up, still nervous.

"What are you, her fat guardian angel?" Maya huffs as her girls snicker.

"Don't worry about it," I snap back. "So, is this your idea of fun, Deb?" I question her.

"Yes," she replies, still in a haze. "I'm not a little goody-two-shoes like you, so leave me alone."

"Looks like she made her decision. So get the hell out of my house before I call security and tell them you are trespassing," Maya threatens.

"Fine. Stay then, but don't come beggin' us to help you when the Sticks kick you to the curb," I warn my girl.

"Who you callin' a stick?" one of them asks.

"You," I snap. "What are you gonna do about it?"

"Let's go, Deb," Robin chimes in, trying to ease the tension in the room. "C'mon, Eboni, let's get her out of here." Deb starts crying as Robin and I grab each arm and help her out of the house.

"You guys are embarrassing me," she screams as we make our way through the party. "I was fine. Where I was."

"Hey!" Juan runs up to us. "What's goin' on? What's wrong with Deb?"

"She's drunk as hell and clearly has lost her mind," I inform him. "Help us."

Juan, Robin, and I finally get her outside and prop her up against a wall. "We can't let her mom see her like this. She's supposed to pick us up in a couple hours," I reason. "We need to get her to sober up."

"I think I'm gonna throw up." Deb sobs, trying to stand on wobbly feet.

"Wait a minute, girlfriend," Juan instructs, stepping out of the way. "Throw-up does not match my outfit."

"Is she okay?" We turn to see G standing behind us.

"Yeah. We're just trying to help her sober up," I offer.

"Well, if you want, I can take you to get coffee or something."

"Thanks," I say, surprised by this sudden turn of events.

"I'll get my car. Meet me at the bottom of the driveway."

"Well, looks like you ladies have got it from here." Juan winks. "No need in all of us missing a good party. I'll call and check in later."

"Thanks, Juanie."

"No more drinks," Robin scolds.

G pulls up and gets out to help Robin and me get Deb in the backseat. "Eboni, you go ahead. I can catch a ride with someone," she says.

"Okay. I'll call you tomorrow." I hop in the front seat of the Accord. "Get home safe, girlfriend."

"You, too," Robin stresses, giving me the eye.

"There's a Starbucks up the block," G informs me, closing my door.

"Great."

After he gets in the car and closes the door on his side, darkness envelops us. My heart starts beating out of control and suddenly I feel hot and sweaty. My throat is dry, too. I watch the muscles in his leg closest to me move up and down when he presses on the accelerator. Even though I want to say something, nothing would come out. "Here's the Starbucks," he says, breaking the silence. "I'll run in and get us three coffees. You want anything special?"

"Regular coffee with cream is fine," I hear myself say. Though I don't like coffee, I can't do anything but smile as he leaves the car. He comes back with three large cups. I hand one to Deb. She takes one sip then falls back asleep, but not before pushing the cup back at me. I take a sip, just because I don't know what else to do.

"Ugh! That's nasty," explodes from my mouth.

"I could've gotten you a hot chocolate." G chuckles. "I wasn't a big coffee drinker either, but when it's cold at the games anything warm will do."

"Well, just being a *fan*," I say sarcastically, "I wouldn't know."

"So you a fan of the mighty G, huh?" His smile broadens.

"No, I'm not! I just said that because that's how you referred to me when you were with your boys after the game."

"Nah," he replies, more serious. "I don't think of you that way. I probably just said that to keep it easy. You seem cool. You remind me of the women in my family—down-to-earth and thick. You know what I mean?"

He glances in the backseat at Deb, who is totally knocked out, then reaches past me, touching my thigh as he pulls out a Mary J CD from the glove compartment and glides it into the CD player. He turns the music down real low and turns to face me. My heart starts beating fast again, and my thigh feels like it's on fire.

"Does Maya remind you of any of the women in your family?" I ask, curious about his attraction to her.

"Not at all. She's cool. Different. It is one of the reasons I hang out with her."

Though I feel a tinge of jealousy, I try to play it cool. "Is that a good thing or a bad thing?"

"It's no thing," he says casually. "I hang with her because she has shown me stuff a brother wouldn't have been exposed to otherwise. She took me horseback-riding once. She also invited me on their family vacation to Greece last year, but my auntie wasn't having it."

"Your aunt, not your mother?"

"It's kinda complicated," he says, looking out of the window. "I live in View Park with my aunt and uncle. I moved there with my moms after my dad died. He was a firefighter. He died in the line of duty a few years ago. My moms had a breakdown after that. She comes around from time to time."

"That's rough," I say sympathetically.

"We've all got something we have to deal with," he says matter-of-factly. "I ultimately want to make the best of my situation by going to the NFL. My goal is to get drafted by the Philadelphia Eagles. It was my pop's favorite team."

"What did you mean by the comment 'You don't seem like you're from around here'?" I ask with a little attitude.

"You just seem like you are more self-assured than most Cali girls. You got a banging body, too." He looks directly at me. "I've never dated a big girl before."

I want to ask if this little coffee break meant we were dating, but I am too nervous to go there. I can tell that whatever G Hicks wants, he gets. But he isn't gonna get me that easy. Boyfriend is gonna have to work if he wants this. Though I couldn't stand some of our previous encounters, being with him now and hearing him open his heart makes me imagine myself wrapped in his big arms and him kissin' me with those beautiful, luscious lips, but I have to control myself.

"Well, I better get you home," he says, starting up his car. A half hour later, we turn onto my street. *Please let my parents be asleep.* Thankfully, when we get in front of my house, it's dark. "You want me to help you get her in?" G offers.

"No, we'll be cool. Thanks for the ride and for the coffee."

"No problem," he says. "Thanks for listening."

"See you at school."

"Peace."

I get Deb up to my room, put her in my other twin bed, and call her mom to tell her that she doesn't have to pick us up and to ask if it's okay if Deb spends the night. Thankfully, she doesn't ask to speak to Deb.

Dear God,
This is gonna be a short one. Tonight was crazy. Thanks for getting us home safely. And for the close encounter with G. Good night.

Chapter 18

E boni, are you awake?" Deb whispers from her bed.

"No," I mumble.

"Then how are you answering me?" There's a pause as she awaits a response.

"Because I'm Superwoman."

"I just wanted to say thanks."

"For what?"

"For getting me out of there last night."

I sit up and glance at her. She's got a blanket pulled all the way up to her chin and tucked around her, like a mummy. "What happened? One minute you were with us and the next you had disappeared."

"The only thing I remember is being at a bonfire talking to this girl from my Spanish class and one of Maya's girls walking up and asking if I wanted to go in the house. I couldn't believe it at first because she's never said more than five words to me before," Deb says, wrinkling her forehead to concentrate. "We ended up in this all-red room and before I knew it, they started smoking from this pipe and passed it to me."

"Did G hit it?"

"I don't think so. He was kinda quiet. When I did, though, my head started spinnin'. That's when one of the guys asked me to kiss him and that's all I remember."

"Did you know him?"

"Not really. But he was cute so I just did it."

"Girl, you're outta control. You realize that, right?"

"I guess I just lost it for a second."

"You lost it for more than a second. The minute we hit the party, you were buggin'," I remind her. "Do you recall what you were doing when Robin and I busted in?"

"No. It's all a blur."

"You had just finished giving one guy a blow job and you were about to hook up another one."

"No I wasn't," she moans.

"Yes you were. Robin and I watched the whole thing go down from the door. Maya and her girls were laughing at you."

"God," she says in agony. "What have I done?"

"Deb, how could you put your mouth on some boy's—" I can't even finish the sentence the thought grosses me out so much. "That's just nasty."

"I know," she says. "When I drink, I guess I get a little wild."

"Then you don't need to be drinkin', especially if it makes you that crazy."

There's a long pause between us. "You're right."

"So, how long have you been doin' it?"

"What?"

"Having sex."

"I lost my virginity last year, but I haven't had sex since then. Just BJs."

This last admission has me wide-awake and puzzled. "Last time I checked blow jobs was having sex, Deb."

"No it's not," she says defensively.

"What's the difference?"

"Sex is when a boy sticks it in."

"Oh, so as long as they're not stickin' it in, then it's cool?"

"Yeah. It's no biggie. And you can't get pregnant."

I stare at Deb.

"What?" she says. "Why're you lookin' at me like that?"

"Because that sounds crazy and it doesn't make sense."

"Sure it does."

"Girl, if a part of your body touches the sex organ of somebody else's, that's sex."

"I don't think so," she says contemplatively. "It's just hookin' up."

"You can catch something whether they stick it in or not."

"God, Eboni. Please don't say that."

"It's true, girl, especially if you're messin' with those nasty jocks. They'll do anything with anybody anywhere."

"Well, you don't have to worry about that ever again."

"Good, 'cause I can't be carrying you out of parties. Your ass is heavy." I giggle, trying to lighten the moment.

"I am not."

"Just kidding. But for real, Deb, later for the Sticks. They aren't cool and they aren't your friends. And I can't believe you were about to kick Robin and me to the curb to kick it with them when we were trying to get you out of there."

"I know. I guess I was just excited when they asked me to hang with them."

"Listen, we may not have phat cribs with tennis courts, and my swimming pool might be the size of Maya's bathtub, but at least we aren't fake and phony."

"You're right."

"Let's make a pact," I suggest.

"What?" she says, sitting up.

"Let's chill for a while and try to be happy with who we are and what we have. No more diets. No more drinking. No more smoking."

"Deal," she says. "I need to chill, anyway."

"Now, c'mon. Let's see what my mom hooked up for breakfast. I'm starving."

From: Michellettc@aol.com
To: Ebonieyesttc@aol.com
Re: Cali Update

Hey E,

Dang girl. Sounds like you got a jones for G again. I'm happy you guys finally connected and cleared the air. Well, I might as well fill you in on my news. Mike and I did it. Girl, it was wild. We were at my house. My mom was on a business trip. I didn't plan to, it just sort of happened. We started out just kissin' and before I knew it, he had my top off. He told me if we did it, it would make us closer. The only thing that worries me is that we didn't use protection. It wasn't like I expected it would be, though. It kinda hurt. After we did it, I wasn't sure we had because it wasn't like I've always imagined it would be and now he's trippin'. And that crazy girl is starting to trip again, too. But you know me. I'm cool. I can handle things. Well E, looks like you're the last virgin in the crew, but judging from your e-mail, maybe not for long.

Love you,
'Chelle

The last part of Michelle's e-mail rocks me. She is havin' a love jones, too. Unlike me, though, she has acted on her feelings, while I am still trying to sort through mine. I feel bad for her that after taking that big step, Mike is acting crazy. I feel crazy, too. Crazy about G. I decide to put on T-Mac's CD and play my favorite song, "Crazy About You." After that, I break out Mary J's CD, the one G played that night in the car.

Dear God,

Everybody around me seems to be wilding out. First Deb. Now 'Chelle. Even though Mom has always said that having sex is something special, not to be offered to someone who won't appreciate it, it still feels like something I want to experience soon. I want to feel love. I want to feel that sensation again of when Vincent kissed me. I want to feel like the sharp points of stars are doing cartwheels across my skin. I just wonder if G is the right one. We had fun talkin' and getting to know each other. I guess I'll just have to see how it goes. He asked for my number (we'll see if he uses it). I hope Michelle and

Mike make it. I can't believe she wasn't smarter about it though, after waiting so long. I would never have sex without a condom. I don't want to even think about the possibility of getting pregnant. Mom and Dad would kill me—and G.

Chapter 19

"**V**ote *Maya Williams* for student council president," Robin and I overhear one of the Sticks tell a group of girls as they hand them flyers.

"Cool," a tall girl with braces says, taking the flyer.

"Can she count on your vote?" one of the Sticks asks another student.

"She can count on whatever she wants from me," a boy with them assures her. "'Cause babygirl is bangin'."

"Great. Wear this pin to show your support?" the Stick with long braids instructs, pinning a jewel-encrusted ribbon with Maya's smiling face on his shirt.

"Did she just say what I think she said?" I ask Robin.

"Sounds like Maya's gonna be your opponent."

"Great," I groan. "This is not cool. Maybe I should just hang it up now."

Robin looks at me and stops dead in her tracks. "You're kidding, right?"

"No," I say, pissed off. "I'm done."

"I still believe in what we're doing," she assures me. "Do you?"

"I guess."

"Listen, Eboni, if this was a popularity contest, Maya would beat you, no doubt about it," Robin exclaims. "Everybody knows her. Everybody wants to be her friend."

"Remind me whose team you're on again," I say as another boy with a smiling Maya pin strolls past us. "Because right now, I'm not feelin' like you're down with Team Imes."

"Don't be silly. Of course I am. But you can't win a popularity contest against one of the most popular girls in school," Robin states matter-of-factly.

"So why am I wasting my time then?"

"Because, this isn't a popularity contest. It's student government. You can beat her on the issues. Trust me, all Maya's good at doing is prancing around campus in her high heels, jumping in and out of cars with boys, and figuring out which designer bag to carry. When she finds out she's gotta attend meetings and determine school policy, you'll get her."

"That's a good point," I concede. "And exactly how do we do that again?"

"I'm working on it," she says, displaying a wicked smile.

"Dang. I can't seem to avoid this girl. Not only do I have to tolerate her fakeness in class and watch her flirt with my man, now I've got to run against her, too. And win."

"Eboni, listen, we've gotta work hard and together we'll do it. That's why you made me your campaign manager, right?"

"Right."

"All right then. It's time to do the damn thing, then."

"What did you just say?" I ask, tickled by her last statement.

"I said, it's time to do the damn thing," she repeats.

"Well, alrighty then."

How does Eboni Michelle Hicks sound?" I inquire of Juan and Deb as we wait for the bus.

"The word 'Hick' never has a ring, especially attached to the name of a star." Juan smirks. "Stars only go by one name. So stick with just Eboni."

"Okay, maybe it doesn't sound like a movie star name, but I'd give up fame for my man," I say, still on a G high. "I can see it now. We'll live in a big house. Have three beautiful children. Two boys and a girl. I'll bring the kids to all of their father's NFL games. That is, of course, after I get home from the set of my Emmy-winning sitcom."

"Okay, sistah. Come on back to reality." Juan waves his hands in my face.

"Stop hatin'."

"Leave her alone, Juan," Deb says supportively.

"Thanks, girlfriend."

"Let her have her dreams."

As we goof off, I spot G's Honda turning the corner. "Yo, is that your boy?" Deb points.

"Yep." I smile, getting up so he sees us. But before I can flag him down, I notice Maya in the passenger seat. G speeds by but not before Maya makes sure to glance in our direction and roll her eyes.

"Are you okay, girlfriend?" Juan asks, sensing my disappointment.

"Yeah." I sigh, face broken once again by G's dis. "I just suddenly really want to beat that girl in the election."

"You will," Juan assures me. "And you'll do it in Prada." As bad as I feel, I still can't help but laugh.

From: Ebonieyesttc@aol.com
To: Michellettc@aol.com
Re: Cali Update

Hey 'Chelle,
Guess who decided to throw her hat in the race for student council president? You guessed it. Maya Williams. That girl bugs me. It isn't like she really cares about doing the work. She has all of her pigeons doing it for her.
    Have things gotten any better for you and Mike?

I am in need of a T-Mac fix, so I scroll through all of his hits and decide to put on the cut "Never Give Up." It has got me pumped up and ready to battle Maya.

Dear God,
What's up with the curveball? I thought G and I had a great conversation. Was I wrong? Was I the only one who felt something, or did he feel it, too? I'm confused. Why would he ask for my number and not use it? And why

would he drive right by me with Maya in the car and not even speak? I guess I can't be mad. He did say in so many words that he was feelin' her, too. I can't compete with Maya. And I don't want to. If G can't see what he's missin', it's not my job to make him.

Chapter 20

From: Michellettc@aol.com
To: Ebonieyesttc@aol.com
Re: Cali Update

H3y GURL,
Mike and I are cool again. Howz the c@mp@ign going?

Luv,
'Chelle

* * *

From: Ebonieyesttc@aol.com
To: Michellettc@aol.com
Re: Cali Update

Wh@t Up M,
Crazy. Maya's crew is supposedly giving out iPods (secretly, of course, and off campus), movie passes, and invites to celebrity parties. As usual, she's got her girls doing all the work. Right now, I don't know how I'm gonna win

this thing, but I've got Deb, Robin, & Juan on the case. Just when I thought I was getting somewhere, 'ole girl has thrown me another curve, but I'm not worried. I will prevail.

* * *

From: Michellettc@aol.com
To: Ebonieyesttc@aol.com
Re: Cali Update

Wow! Y'all doin' big things out West. iPods? Passes to movie premieres? So, wh@t's UR pl@n?

* * *

From: Ebonieyesttc@aol.com
To: Michellettc@aol.com
Re: Cali Update

I don't h@ve one yet. @ny ideas? I need something big. Something that'll get it poppin' for me and get people excited.

* * *

From: Michellettc@aol.com
To: Ebonieyesttc@aol.com
Re: Cali Update

Well, E, your family owns a Mickey D's. Hook up something there!!!

From: Ebonieyesttc@aol.com
To: Michellettc@aol.com
Re: Cali Update

Yo! That's a great idea, 'Chelle!!!! I can't believe I didn't
think of it!!!! Thanks girl. I'll keep you posted.

∗ ∗ ∗

From: Michellettc@aol.com
To: Ebonieyesttc@aol.com
Re: Cali Update

Sure. You gotta represent for the TTC. Do it big, gurl. Your
opponent may be rich, but she ain't the only hottie on that
campus. Clearly they ain't knowin' who Eboni Michelle
Imes is.

michelle's idea to use our restaurant is a good one. It has
never occurred to me that I could perhaps do something
there.

Hey, Daddy."
    "Hey there, baby girl."
    "I need your help."
    "Shoot," he says, taking a break from his paperwork,
putting down his pen, and turning his attention to me.
    "Well, you know I've decided to run for student council
president, right?"

"Yes, Mom filled me in on things. I think that's great."

"Well, my campaign is weak right now. I need something to get people to vote for me."

"Okay."

"I was thinking maybe I could do a giveaway at the restaurant."

"A giveaway, huh?" he says, letting the idea sink in.

"Yes. My opponent is hardly qualified for the job. She's just *rich*," I stress, hoping that additional bit of information will persuade him. "She's got fancy campaign pins and she's giving away iPods and movie premiere passes."

"I see," Dad says. "That's pretty big. And you think a giveaway at the restaurant will do the trick?"

"Well, it's a start," I reason. "I mean everybody has to eat, and I don't know anyone who doesn't love McDonald's. It could be my chance to meet more of my classmates and inform them of my plans to improve the school."

"And exactly what is your plan?"

"My slogan is 'It's Time for a Change,'" I say. "What do you think of that?"

"I like that, honey."

"I figure since I'm the outsider trying to come into the whole Beacon Hills thing, I can make some changes to make things better."

"Well, we've definitely got to figure out a way for you to have your party," he says. "Let me talk it over with Corey."

"Cool. Thanks, Dad. I knew you'd understand." I plant a kiss on his smooth, bald head.

"Sure, baby girl. Now, let me get back to this paperwork

so I can figure out how to pay for all this free food you want us to give away."

"Okay. I've got homework, anyway. 'Night."

"Good night. Sleep tight," he says, returning to his pile of papers. "Oh, one more thing."

"Yes?"

"I'm proud of you."

"I'm proud of you, too, Daddy."

Dear God,
It's me again. Before I start asking for stuff, let me just say thanks for giving me a wonderful life. I love Mommy, Daddy, Corey, and Yvette. I also love my crew. I don't know what You have in store for me, for the election, or for my meet and greet, but I pray it all works out.

maya *probably figures* her party was so off-the-hook she can chill," Robin says as we work on the details of my upcoming meet and greet.

Deb has typed up a flyer listing all the details, Robin got her mom to make copies at her job, and Juan has pulled together an outfit for me to wear. We flood the campus with flyers urging everyone to come out. By now, a lot of the students have seen my posters and know my name. "Okay, so the plan is that anyone who shows a valid school ID will get a free order of French fries."

"We'll have a table set up so people can come by and pick up information on your campaign plan," Robin says.

"Sounds good."

"Tomorrow's the day. You ready?" Deb asks.

"Yep."

By the time I lay my head down on the pillow, the next day arrives. I am nervous and excited at the same time. I carefully put on the clothes Juan has selected for me, paying attention to every detail. I slip the pink halter dress over my head and tie the knot securely. I snap on my Tiffany bracelet with the heart-shaped charm, then put on the matching toggle necklace. To finish the outfit off, I add a pair of low-heeled, pink-and-green-plaid mules. I'm pleased when I look in the mirror and add a touch of clear MAC Lipglass. There is no way G will be able to resist me when he shows up to the meet and greet.

You are workin' that outfit, Miss E."

"But you put it together."

"I know. That's why I love it," Juan says, stepping toward me. "I'm da bomb."

"Whatever, boy." I grin, checking out the table. "I think I'm nervous."

"You'll be fine. Sorry I can't stay. My mom's been planning my brother's party for months."

"I understand. Go have fun. You've definitely hooked me up."

"Well, these are for you, too." He hands me a box with a ribbon around it.

"What's this?"

"Open it."

"Chocolate lollipops?"

"Yeah. They're from this place called See's Candies. Check out the ribbon."

"'Don't Be a Sucker, Vote Eboni Imes for Student Council President,'" I read. "I love it. Thank you, honey bunny."

"Can you hook up a chocolate shake for the road? A girl is parched." He coughs.

"Sure. Coming up."

The meet and greet was to be from two until five o'clock. Throughout the day, a steady stream of customers came in the restaurant. Some noticed the sign and came over. Others made donations. Mr. Hinds stopped by to wish me luck, but by four only two students had shown up—one was the nerd from my math class, who was more interested in the free fries than talking to me. The other was a girl who seemed obsessed with my plan to change cheerleader tryouts. Though I was grateful for their support, it was gonna take more than their two votes to win.

"Okay y'all, if this is a sign of what's to come, I think we're in trouble," I tell Robin and Deb.

"We still have a shot."

"Robin, you've got to be the most optimistic person I know. But I'm a realist. This didn't work."

"You never know," she says.

I appreciate my girl's enthusiasm, and instead of arguing, I decide to chill.

"What's goin' on here?" a man inquires, approaching the table.

"My name is Eboni Imes. I'm running for student council president at Beacon Hills High," I say to the handsome black man in the business suit. "The election is next week."

"I see," he says, picking up a flyer. "Looks like you've got some good suggestions here. How's it going?"

"Not too good. Only three people showed up and one was my debate teacher."

"Well, hang in there. Here's a donation," he says, handing me a fifty-dollar bill. "Good luck."

"Wow, thanks."

"Make sure you put it to good use."

"Oh, she will," Robin chimes in. "As her campaign manager, I'll make sure."

"It's good to see young people trying to make a positive difference. You're about the same age as my client when he got started in the business."

"Who's your client?"

"The singer T-Mac."

I feel faint. "Did you say T-Mac? As in 'Mr. Entertainment?'"

"That's cute." He chuckles. "Yes. I'm his attorney."

"Ohmigod. Ohmigod. I love him so much."

"My dad's an attorney," Deb says.

"What's your dad's name?"

"Howard Goldstein."

"I know your father very well. We worked together on a case a few years ago."

"My name is Eboni Michelle Imes," I repeat, forgetting about the name tag stuck to my dress and too excited to care, since this man can get me next to T-Mac. "Can you please tell him I love him?"

"He's performing here next week. Would you like to tell him yourself?"

"For real?" My eyes light up.

"Tell you what." He turns to Deb and hands her a business card. "Have your dad call my office. Maybe we can arrange to get you ladies tickets to the show."

"I sure will," she says, tucking it into her pocket.

"Oh, we also have another friend, Juan, who isn't here. He'd kill us if we forgot him."

"No problem. Tell your father John Leonard said hello and I look forward to his call," he says to Deb. "It's nice to meet you, ladies. Good luck with the election."

"Thank you, Mr. Leonard," I say, thrilled, as he walks out the door. "Okay, meeting him more than makes up for the dry turnout."

"It was pretty pathetic," Robin finally concedes. "But I still feel good about this thing."

"Deb, please don't forget to have your father call Mr. Leonard first thing Monday morning. We've got to be in the house for that show."

"Don't worry, girl. I'm gonna tell him as soon as I get home."

Robin doesn't seem to be in the same T-Mac frenzy that's got Deb and me buzzin'. "You okay, Robin?"

"Yeah, I'm cool."

"What's on your mind?"

"Nothing. Just trying to figure out what our next move should be."

"What are you thinking?"

"I don't know yet."

"'Cause all I can think about right now is seeing T-Mac in concert."

Dear God,

Well, the campaign party is over. It definitely didn't turn out the way I had hoped. This election is way harder than I thought it would be. Maybe since it was a Saturday, people had better things to do. The highlight was meeting T-Mac's attorney. I can't believe I may actually see him in concert. That would be da bomb and it would take my mind off what I've gotten myself into.

You never cease to amaze me. Just when I thought we should pack up and go, here comes T-Mac's attorney with the opportunity to meet him. How cool is that. Thanks.

Chapter 21

Yo, Deb, what's going on?"

"Have you been online, today?"

"No. I had to study for three tests, finalize my speech, and work at the restaurant. I just walked in," I inform her, kicking off my laceless Converse and falling out on the bed.

"I got a text from Juan. He happened to be checkin' out Maya's MySpace page and said she posted a blog about us."

"What?" I sit up in a panic. "What does it say?"

"It reads. And I quote, 'talk about losers . . . two uninvited guests (or should I say pests) got totally wasted at my birthday party and gave some players on the football team blow jobs." Deb shrieks. "'The thin wannabe and her fat friend totally played themselves. I guess that's what happens when you're total losers trying to fit in.'"

"Why's she buggin'?" I ask, pissed by this new brewing mess. "One of the Sticks gave me an invite and Maya even spoke to me when I was talking to G."

"She's probably mad because you broke up her private party with G."

"I didn't ask him to bring us home. He came out and volunteered."

"I know. But whatever Maya wants Maya gets, and she wants G."

"Well, she should take that up with him. 'Cause I ain't got nuthin' to do with that, and I don't appreciate her puttin' my name in some bull that isn't true."

"I hear you." Deb sighs. "What should we do?"

"We need to get her skinny, crazy ass in check."

"Let's just let it go. Hopefully nobody'll see it and this'll all blow over."

"Are you crazy, Deb? I'm not lettin' anything go. It's a straight-up lie and I'm not goin' for it. I don't need this drama while I'm trying to win an election."

"This is all my fault." She sobs. "If I hadn't gotten drunk, this never would've happened. I'm sorry, Eboni."

"Deb, look. Don't stress about it anymore. The party's over."

"Well, do you want me to talk to her?"

"I don't know yet, but I'm not about to have people thinkin' I'm givin' boys blow jobs when I'm not. What if my mother read that? Maya and her bony cronies have gone too far this time and she's not getting away with it."

"Well, whatever you decide, I got your back."

"Thanks," I say, trying to remain calm.

"Talk to you later, girl."

"Yeah, later."

After we hang up, I go over and turn on my computer to check out Maya's MySpace page for myself. When I find it and read each lying line, it's hard to remain calm. I'm sure

Maya put one of the Sticks up to doin' her dirty work, and if I try confronting them, they'd only protect her. To correct this situation, I am gonna have to go to the "Queen Bee" herself. And that's definitely going to require some restraint. Before I can print a copy, Juan calls.

"So, have you seen it?"

"Yep, Deb just called and told me about it."

"So, what do you plan to do?"

"I don't know, but trust me. It's gonna get handled."

"Don't do anything rash, *mamacita*. Sleep on it. But if we need to beat that broad down, I got your back."

"Thanks, Juan. I'll let you know."

Dear God,

I'm pissed. Why does my name have to be mixed up in some scandalous stuff that doesn't even concern me? The only thing I tried to do was help my girl out, now Maya is spreading lies that are gonna have people thinkin' that I'm doing stuff that I'm not, especially in the middle of this election. This is crazy. I can't understand why we just can't get along. She's a black girl and so am I. So what if we come from different parts of the country. What I really want to do is kick Maya's skinny butt to the curb, but all that'll do is get me suspended. Give me strength not to go off on this girl when I see her, because right now, I really want to fight her.

On the way to third period, Deb and I spot Maya alone—a rarity, since she and the Sticks usually travel in a pack. "You ready?" Deb asks.

"As ready as I'm gonna be." We follow Maya into the bathroom. Though I want to squash this situation, it's still a little nerve-wracking. "Hi, Maya," I say, leaning on the sink when she exits the stall.

"Hi," she says curtly, going to the sink to wash her hands.

"I'd like to talk to you for a minute."

"About what?"

"About the bogus blog on your MySpace page?"

"I don't know what you're talking about," she says, digging in a Fendi bag.

"I thought you'd say that, so I printed up a copy." I throw the paper in her direction. She glances at it briefly, then starts primping in the mirror.

"I said I don't know anything about it," she repeats.

"I find that hard to believe."

"Oh well," she snipes.

"How can you not know anything about it and it's on your page?" I press, starting to get pissed that she's trying to play me.

"Maybe it's not my real page. Maybe somebody made it up."

"Somebody like one of your flunkies."

"I don't have flunkies."

"Listen. I really don't care what you call your friends. All I want to know is what's with all the hate? What have I ever done to you? You don't even know me, yet you're ready to dog me. I'm a black girl just like you. We should be friends, not enemies," I say, exasperated.

Maya looks at me long and hard for a minute. "Look, I

don't have time for these games. I said I didn't do it and I don't know who did. Now leave me alone." She makes her way toward the door.

"I know what this is about."

"What?" She swings around. "What is it about?"

"It's about G Hicks."

"What about him?"

"You're just pissed because he left your party to take us home. I know it's hard for you to believe he's feelin' me," I stress. "But he is."

"Oh, please." She laughs. "After he took you and your pathetic little friend home, he came back to the party and continued where we left off."

She threw me off with that one. "I don't even know why I'm trying to reason with you." I throw my hands up in despair. "Look, Maya, I really don't care why you and your crew posted the fake blog. All I care about is you removing it, or you'll be sorry."

"Are you threatening me?" she asks, looking me up and down.

"Call it what you want. But you don't want me to expose how you've been buying votes."

"Listen, you don't scare me." She laughs. "You can't prove anything. If I want to give away iPods and passes to hot parties, there's nothing you can do about it. Now, if you don't mind. I have to get to class."

"Fine," I say, satisfied that I had made my point.

She sashays away and attempts to open the door. "Did you lock me in here?"

"Maybe."

This is the first time she looks nervous. But after struggling a bit, she gets the door open and leaves. Our exchange has me so drained all I can do is turn on the faucet and sprinkle water on my face. "Did you get it?"

"Got it," Deb says, pushing open the bathroom closet door and pressing stop on her camcorder. "This is all the evidence we need to take her down."

"Good. Because I can't take much more of this Maya mess."

I don't think you should do it," Robin says when Deb and I play the tape for her.

"Why?" Deb asks, perplexed. "This will prove she's buying the election."

"Because I think Eboni can win without exposing her. All that tape will do is show that you two set her up. It might even backfire if the principal gets involved."

Deb and I have been so focused on getting Maya to confess that we never considered the consequences of our actions. "You don't want to win like that, do you?"

"Robin, I appreciate all the positive energy, but in case you forgot, two people showed up at the meet and greet."

"I know. I was there. But you've got to stay positive. Take the high road."

Deep down, I know Robin is right, and I am so stressed I don't have the strength to fight anymore. "You're right, Robin. I guess we just got caught up. Deb, did your dad call that attorney?"

"Yep. We're on for the concert."

"When is it?"

"Tomorrow night."

"All of us?" I ask.

"Yeah. I sent you a text. You didn't get it?"

"I must've missed it with all of this going on. If anybody can make me feel better, it's my baby, T-Mac."

Dear God,

Getting Maya to confess was exactly what we needed to expose her as the evil cheater that she is. That much is true. But it didn't feel right ambushing her in the way we did. I know Deb's intentions were to help, but I never should've gone along with the idea. I guess I felt desperate. Seeing her house, all those kids in her backyard, and everyone jockin' her made me feel like I didn't have a shot at winning this election. I shouldn't hate on her because she's been blessed to live the way she does. I just need to focus on my blessings and the wonderful things You've given my family. We aren't rich, but we definitely are blessed. I hope what we did doesn't ruin my run. Robin was right. I've got to take the high road. If it's for me, I will have it. If not, at least I'll feel good about the fact that I didn't play myself to win.

Chapter 22

I *couldn't decide* what to wear to the biggest concert of my life. It was one thing to read every article about T-Mac, to have his fine face plastered all over my room, own all of his CDs, and know all the words to his songs, but quite another to actually be up close and personal with the man.

He had pretty much gotten me through my first few months in Los Angeles. During my G jones, I downloaded his video with Alicia Keys on my iPod and fantasized about it being me and G. That was before G dismissed me as "a fan." After that, I played "Hate on Me" so many times Mom came in to see if something was wrong with my CD player. I also wore out "Be Mine" from T-Mac's *This Is the Way It Is* CD. None of that mattered now, though, because I'd decided to say later for G.

"Hey, E," Deb calls to check in.

"Hey."

"You ready?"

"Almost," I say, resting the cordless phone against my shoulder to search through the closet for my favorite jean jacket. "I'm tellin' you now if T-Mac looks at me, I'm gonna probably faint."

"I'll try to catch you but I can't guarantee it."

"You don't know how many times I played his song 'Blaze.'"

"Yes I do. A million."

"Don't let me make a fool of myself in front of my future husband."

"Dad and I will honk in about ten minutes."

"Cool. I'll be ready."

*C*limb in, troops," Mr. Goldstein instructs as we hop into the backseat of his silver Mercedes-Benz. "We've got a hot show to get to." The entire ride, everyone's buzzing, but I can't even speak, I'm so excited.

"You okay, E?" Juan elbows me.

"Yeah, girl, why are you so quiet? I thought you'd be going crazy," Robin says.

"I am. Inside, my stomach is in knots." This was by far the biggest thrill of my move. Bigger than the swimming pool. Bigger even than seeing Beacon Hills for the first time.

"All right, kids. This should be fun," Mr. Goldstein says, looking hip in a pair of Levi's and expensive loafers. Though I don't see much of him, Mr. Goldstein is cool.

"Tickets for Goldstein," he says, sliding his driver's license to a clerk.

"Yes, sir," a young blond woman replies, handing him an envelope. "Enjoy the show."

"Oh, we will, right, guys?" He hands us VIP badges. "Put these on and keep them on until the show starts."

"What does 'all access' mean exactly?" I whisper to Juan.

"It means we can go to a VIP area where there's usually food and drinks, maybe a few celebrities."

When we get to the VIP area, everyone looks so chic. As usual, most of the women are thin, with flawless skin. I've seen so many weaves since arriving in Cali that I have become an expert at detecting them, and most of the women here have them.

"Wait here, kids. I want to let John know we're here."

"Okay, Dad."

"Yo, is that Ciara?" I inquire, noticing a pretty girl in parachute pants and heels posing for a picture.

"I think so," Robin says, trying to get a better look.

"And that looks like Lil Jon with her."

"Heck, yeah, that's Miss Ciara," Juan observes. "You know girlfriend's from the ATL like T-Mac, so is Lil Jon, that's probably why they're here. . . . She's tall," Juan notices.

"And pretty," Deb adds. "Alicia Keys, too."

"Where?" I scream, whipping around to find her.

"Okay, first of all I'm gonna need you to chill," Juan scolds. "Stop actin' like you aren't from here."

"But I'm not."

"Okay, well, then, act like you are. Play it cool, like me. Even though I'm about to pee in my pants because I love me some Alicia Keys, you don't see me talking loud and drawing attention to myself."

"Okay, sorry."

"She's right over there." Juan jerks his head in Alicia's direction.

"Ooh, I see her now. Wow, you're right. She is pretty. I wonder if she's gonna do that duet with T-Mac? That's my ultimate jam."

"Mine, too," Juan says. "'Cause girlfriend was laid out in that video. I bet the fur alone was at least a hundred Gs."

"I dare you to go over there and introduce yourself."

"You think I'm scared?" Juan says defiantly.

"Yep."

"Watch this diva go over and greet that one."

"I can't believe him. He's really doing it."

After a few minutes, Alicia hugs Juan like they're old friends. He then reaches into his pocket and pulls out his cell phone and snaps a picture of the two of them cheek-to-cheek. "Ohmigod. He's taking a picture with her." They hug again and he rejoins us.

"Okay, girls, Alicia Keys may have just replaced Beyoncé as my favorite diva," Juan gushes as he checks out the photo.

"Let me see that," I shout, grabbing the phone out of his hand.

"Girlfriend is cool as hell."

"What did you say to her?" I ask, interested in how one talks to celebs.

"I just said 'I love your music and one day you gonna be sportin' my designs.'"

"What did she say?"

"She said that if they're anything like what I'm rockin'

now, she can't wait." He laughs, poppin' the collar on his rhinestone-studded shirt.

Juan and I continue to stargaze as Deb and Robin chat.

"Okay, guys, John wants to know if you want to meet T-Mac before he goes onstage," Mr. Goldstein announces.

At that moment, my heart starts to thump. "Brace yourself, baby," Juan says, sensing my excitement. "Breathe."

"We can only go in for a few minutes, say hello, and then take our seats."

At that moment, all I can do is grab Mr. Goldstein. "Thank you." I hug him. "I love you."

"Well." He smiles, surprised. "I guess that's a yes for Eboni."

They all laugh, but I don't care. This is big.

"Well, then, shall we?"

Mr. Goldstein leads us backstage, where a group of dancers and members of T-Mac's band are preparing for the show. I notice three pretty girls zipping up costumes. "How's my hair?" I ask Juan, fingering through it to make sure it's cool.

"It looks great," he says, referring to the long, straight bob I'd been growing.

"You look good, too," I offer nervously.

We approach a door with T-Mac's name in the middle of a star. "Hey, John, here we are."

"Hey, kids. Good to see you again," Mr. Leonard greets us.

"We wouldn't have missed this for the world," Juan says.

"Yeah, thanks for the tickets, Mr. Leonard," Robin adds.

"I think you can go in now. Let me just check," he says, knocking lightly on the door and sticking his head in. It's unbelievable that the only thing that separates me from T-Mac is that door. "Come on in, guys," Mr. Leonard says, pushing the door open.

I imagined T-Mac's dressing room full of groupies and his boys chillin' before the show. But it isn't like that at all when we enter. Aside from a huge flower arrangement, a spread of fruit and cheese, and bottles of Evian, it's just T-Mac and a barber who's lining up his hair. "Hey, guys," he greets us. "Come on in."

"Hey," we all reply in unison.

"So, who do we have here, John?"

"Hi there, Mr. Mac, I'm Howard Goldstein. This is my daughter, Deb," he says, putting his arm around her, "and her friends Juan, Robin, and Eboni, who may just be your biggest fan." Though it is true, it is more than a little embarrassing that Mr. Goldstein has put me on blast like that.

"Is that right?" he says, looking directly at me.

"Yes." I smile, still in shock.

"Well, I appreciate that. I always love meeting my fans."

"So, T, is it okay if the kids take a couple of pictures with you?" Mr. Leonard asks, trying to move things along.

"Sure." He spins around to check out his fresh cut in the mirror.

"Baby, you look perfect. Don't change a thing," I say, surprising myself. Everybody in the room laughs, including T-Mac.

"Okay, why don't you all go over and stand beside T and I'll take a few shots," Mr. Leonard instructs.

T-Mac's diamond stud earring and smooth skin are even more gorgeous up close. He smells wonderful, too. *Note to self: Make sure to find a sample of his cologne next time I'm at the mall to relive this moment again and again.*

"So, how're you doing?" He smiles, putting his arm around me. What I really want to say is, *I'm melting*, but I play it cool, like Juan taught me.

"Great," I respond, looking at him close up.

"Thanks for coming to the show."

"You don't know how long I've wanted to meet you," I confess.

"Okay, everybody, on three say cheese," Mr. Leonard says. "One. Two. Three." When he snaps, the flash is so bright, I'm sure I blinked. "I'll take one more just for insurance."

Thank you, Lord.

He takes another picture and this time I make sure to look straight ahead and focus. "Okay, that looks great."

I didn't think my night could get any better until T-Mac says, "John, take one with just Eboni and me." Everybody, including me, looks at him in disbelief.

"Really?"

"Sure. It's the least I could do for my biggest fan."

I can't believe T-Mac and me together after all these years, and I can't wait to e-mail these photos back home to the crew. They are gonna die, kinda like I am right now. As we stand together, I want to tell him how much I admire him. Aside from the fact that he can dance his butt off, I love that he has performed on Broadway, and that he is helping people affected by Hurricane Katrina. Though I read that his mom got him into show business, I want to ask how he managed to stay on top, since it's my dream to be in entertainment someday, too. But none of the questions come. All I can do is bask in this moment as my heartbeat struggles to return to normal.

"Okay, Eboni, get close," Mr. Leonard says. I move closer and try not to look too starstruck.

"Oh, c'mon, you can do better than that," T teases me. "Get closer. I won't bite."

Before I know it, he's slipped both of his arms around my waist and puts his cheek to mine. My eyes light up as Juan, Deb, and Robin egg us on. "Well, all right." Juan grins. "I may need to get a picture, too." He pulls out his cell phone and snaps a few shots. But it's on the last one that something incredible happens. T-Mac turns and kisses me on the cheek. "Oh my goodness. Thanks," I gush, reeling from the surprise peck.

"You're welcome." He winks. "Thank you for your support, it means a lot."

"Well, T-Mac, thank you. This was awfully nice of you to do before the show," Mr. Goldstein says, handing him an envelope. "This is for your charity."

"Thank you very much. It was my pleasure."

"Okay, kids, we better get to our seats and let Mr. Mac finish getting ready. John," Mr. Goldstein says, shaking Mr. Leonard's hand. "Thanks again, my friend."

"No problem, Howard. I'll make arrangements to get the photos to you."

"Great."

"Have a great show," I say to T-Mac as we leave.

"Thanks. Good luck to you, too."

"On what?"

"I heard about the election. Good luck with it."

I can't believe T-Mac knows about the election and is wishing me luck.

From: Ebonieyesttc@aol.com
To: Michellettc@aol.com
Re: Cali Update

Hey 'Chelle,

Okay, girl, this one is big! Are you ready? I just came back from T-Mac's concert tonight. We had front-row seats. It was incredible. It was a benefit concert for his charity. He sang all his hits, of course. We were getting our party on. But, girl, when he got his cut "You're My Star," he invited me up onstage. I couldn't get up there fast enough. Okay, bump what I said before, I'm lovin' my L.A. life. The only thing that would've made this night better is if you, Charisse, and Yolanda were in the front row with me.

Oh, and on the G front, I'm over him and his games.

Hit me back when you can.

Love,

E

Dear God,
Thanks for such a great night. I will never forget it. I want
to pray that the assembly goes well. I've done the best I
can. I don't think I've ever wanted anything as much as I
want to win this election.

Chapter 23

*Attention, students. Please take a moment to stop by elec-
tion headquarters located on the third-floor patio. This
will be your last chance to meet the candidates before
this afternoon's special assembly. Remember, voting is a
right, not a privilege. Thank you.*

The special assembly is hours away. Though people
haven't shown up for the meet and greet, the patio is buzzing
with students who seem interested in hearing more about
what the candidates have to say. I am pleasantly surprised
when so many people wish me luck and tell me they plan to
vote for me.

I had memorized my speech but decided to put it on
index cards, anyway—just in case. Thanks to debate class
and some helpful advice from Mr. Hinds, I feel good about
my speech. "So, this is it," Robin says, checking out the other
candidates' booths.

"Yep. Finally."

I look for Maya's booth and notice a couple of her girls talking to students. "I don't believe it."

"What?"

"The Sticks are runnin' Maya's booth."

"Are you surprised?"

"I guess not."

"Just remember what I told you."

"I know. If I get nervous, just imagine everyone in their underwear."

"Exactly. I'll be the one in the sexy Victoria's Secret matching leopard bra and panties."

As Robin and I chat, three girls approach the table. "Hi." I extend my hand. "Eboni Imes." The tall one, a brunette, shakes my hand, but the others just stand there. "Thanks for stopping by my table. I'd love your vote for student council president."

A redhead with freckles picks up a few flyers. "Why should we vote for you?"

"Well," I start. "What did you think about the homecoming dance this year?"

"It sucked," the brunette concedes.

"Exactly. I guarantee next year's dance will be slammin'."

"How you gon' do that?" the third one, with a heavy accent, asks.

"You'll have to vote for her to find out," Robin chimes in.

"What else?" the tall one continues.

"Well, here is my list of initiatives." I hand each of them

flyers. "What I can tell you is that I have some definite ideas about how to make Beacon Hills more inclusive. I'm from Baltimore and when I got here, I felt like an outsider."

"Right," the one with the accent agrees. "I'm from Noo Yawk. It's mad crazy out here. They ain't got no flava."

"Vote for me and that'll change. In fact, my slogan is"—I point to the sign—"'It's Time for a Change.' Even though we live in Cali, everything shouldn't revolve around the West Coast. Some of us are from other parts of the world and we've got great ideas."

"True dat," the New Yorker says. "That's what I'm talkin' 'bout."

"I also plan to talk to the head of the girls' athletic department to see if they will change the strict requirements for the drill team and cheerleading squad, and see if we can get the band to improve the song list during the games."

"Sounds good," the tall one utters.

"Well, we'll see you at assembly. Good luck," the redhead offers.

"Thanks. And help yourselves to a lollipop." I gesture toward the See's suckers left over from the first meet and greet. They each grab lollipops and move on.

O*kay, this is it, E. Do you need anything?"* Robin asks.

"No. I think I'm good."

"Oh, before you go up, we've got a surprise for you," Deb informs me as Juan adjusts the collar on the outfit he has dressed me in, a simple, navy blue skirt suit with a sheer white blouse and a red flower in the lapel, for flair.

"This is no time for surprises."

Robin hands me an index card.

"What's this?"

"Just read what it says after you're finished with your speech."

I glance at the lone card but don't really focus on the words. "The last thing I want to do is embarrass myself in front of the entire school."

"Would we let you do that?" Robin questions.

"No, but . . ."

Before I can finish my sentence, I hear the principal, a short, pudgy, balding man in a three-piece suit with buttons that look like they're hanging on for dear life, call my name. "Our final candidate is Miss Eboni Imes."

"Well, here goes."

After calming my nerves and saying a quick prayer, I walk out on stage and glance back at the crew one last time. Robin and Deb give me a thumbs-up as Juan snaps his fingers for me to work it. "Good afternoon," I begin, glancing out at the audience, where I immediately spot Mr. Hinds, who is looking up at me with a reassuring grin. The Sticks are a few rows behind him. "For those of you who don't know me, and I hope by now that's not many, my name is Eboni Imes."

My heart feels like it's about to explode, but I recall Robin's advice. It works, because I glance at the nerd from my algebra class and imagine him in long johns, which makes me chuckle inside. "You may be asking yourself, 'Why should I vote for her?' Great question. For me, this election is about much more than just winning a popularity contest. It's about getting involved and making this a better Beacon Hills for everyone, especially people like me who may not be from California."

I look up to see if people are paying attention, and spot G and some of the other jocks, but they don't even faze me. "You should vote for me because I care about the things that concern you. Your issues will become mine and I will work hard to make a difference." I shuffle through my cards. "During this campaign, I've listened to your concerns and feel confident that by working with other members of student council, I can make a positive difference. One thing I would like to do is bring you the most exciting homecoming ever." A few people applaud. Trying to read from my cards seems too cumbersome, so I decide to speak from the heart. "I am also proposing a universal membership card that offers discounts during basketball and football games, special offers at the student store, and at some of your favorite stores throughout the city. By flashing this card, you'll also have access to music and movie premieres and receive special e-mail promotions, discount coupons, and other perks." This really seems to get the crowd excited. "Of course, all of this will take work and a tireless effort on the part of your student representatives, and I pledge that if given an opportunity to serve, you will be informed every step of the way via my weekly blog. Thank you for listening," I say, wrapping up, before looking down and noticing the index card Robin handed me before I went onstage.

"Oh, and here to tell you a little more is a friend of mine," I utter, looking at them, confused.

The lights go down and a video screen comes on. Just like

everyone else, I can't wait to see who will appear. Suddenly, T-Mac's fine face pops up. "Yo Beacon Hills, what's poppin'?" he starts as the auditorium erupts into wild cheers. "It's your boy T-Mac, and I'm here to tell you about a young lady who will make a wonderful representative for your school. I'm talking about my girl, Eboni Imes. If you want a candidate with integrity who will get the job done, then vote Eboni Imes student council president. Peace." He smiles, holding up two fingers as the screen fades to black.

I'm literally speechless as the auditorium, still reeling from this surprise, begins to settle down. "Well." I grin, dizzy with excitement. "There's nothing more to say after that except 'Vote Eboni Imes student council president.' Thank you."

I grab my notes and dash off the stage to the crew, who are waiting in the wings. "Ohmigod, how'd you guys get T-Mac to do that?" I scream, about to lose it.

"It was actually Deb's idea," Robin explains.

"I asked my dad and he and Mr. Leonard got it done," she says.

"Thank you so much. I love you guys." I grab my three friends and offer up a group hug as we celebrate the end of the campaign and the beginning of what we hope will be a victory. "I couldn't have done any of this without each of you."

"My pleasure, *mamacita*," Juan says. "I was born for this."

"You should've seen Maya and the Sticks when T-Mac's face popped up on that screen. Girl, it was priceless," Robin shares. "I wish I had my camera."

"Really? Good." I grin, completely satisfied.

"Did you notice how Ryan Schwartz was checkin' you out?" Deb asks.

"Who?"

"The hottie runnin' for vice president."

"You guys are trippin'. That boy wasn't checkin' for me."

"Oh, yes he was, missy," Juan interjects. "I think boyfriend has the feva."

"Whatever."

"Another fine performance, Miss Imes," Mr. Hinds says, approaching us.

"Thanks, Mr. Hinds. I'm too excited."

"You should be. I'd be excited, too, if I had one of the hottest singers in the industry singing my praises. That was really something."

"My campaign committee surprised me with that one."

"Well, you've got a great team."

"It's up to the students now," I tell him. "I hope they make the right decision."

"Regardless, you did a great job."

"I want to thank you," I express, feeling a bit emotional. "If it weren't for you, I probably never would've done this, but I'm so glad I did."

"Excuse me," Deb grumbles.

"I meant if it weren't for you *and* the crew," I correct the faux pas.

"Get some rest, because I smell a victory."

"I will."

"Hey, Eboni." I turn to see Ryan Schwartz. "Great speech," he says, reaching to shake my hand.

"Thanks," I say, placing my hand in his. "You, too."

"I hope we get to work together next semester."

"Me, too," I say, noticing for the first time how cute Ryan is.

The crew witnesses our exchange and gives me "told you so" glances. "You believe us now?" Robin beams.

"He was just being nice."

"Whatever, E."

"Hey there, B-More." I turn around again to see G standing behind me.

"Hi." After all that we've been through, that's all I feel compelled to say.

"I just wanted to say good luck. Your speech was bangin'." A few months ago, a compliment like that from Gene Hicks would've sent me to heaven, but now, it means little. I deserve someone who doesn't play games, someone who likes me for me.

"Thanks," I say, before turning back to the crew.

"So, you divas ready to celebrate or what?" Juan asks.

"I'd love to, but I'm exhausted. I just wanna chill tonight and prepare for tomorrow. You guys should, too. You've worked hard."

"*We've* worked hard," Robin corrects.

"You're right. I just want to reflect on today. I promise, I'm gonna treat y'all to some sushi after this is over."

"Sounds like a plan," Juan says. "All that designing has got me whipped, anyway."

Though *Michelle's expecting* an update, all I have the energy to do is check e-mails and go to Beacon Hills's Web site and cast a vote for myself. Just seeing my name and photo on the computer screen next to Maya's makes me giddy. I have finally stepped it up in Cali, and it feels great.

> *Dear God,*
> *What a day. Then again, You know all about my day because You designed it. I can't believe the assembly and what the crew pulled off. I felt like a rock star when the lights went down and T-Mac came up on the screen and endorsed my campaign in front of the entire school. That was big! It was all too much, but all so fly at the same time! Now that the campaign part is over, the nerve-racking part begins. I can honestly say, regardless of the outcome, I am proud of myself, and the job we did to make this campaign a success. I'm also glad that I stayed positive and didn't let all that stuff that happened with Maya derail me from what is important—winning honestly. Thank You for giving me wisdom and for always being there whenever I need You, even though it may take me a while to get it sometimes. Good night!*

Chapter 24

Today's the big day." Mom smiles from her usual morning spot.

"It's out of my hands now," I say, grabbing a plate. "Like you always say, if you're gonna worry, don't pray, and if you're gonna pray, don't worry."

"You're right about that, baby."

It wasn't just the election that had me peaceful. It was also the journey getting to it. "I feel so much lighter now that I realize that whatever my destiny is, it is."

"We can't change what is meant to be. All we can do is take it as it comes and enjoy it."

"That's what I plan to do from now on," I say, scooping some of Mom's homemade cinnamon-raisin oatmeal into a bowl.

"We're all so very proud of you. Daddy and Corey left you notes in the dining room, and Yvette called last night after you went to bed to wish you luck."

After breakfast, I go into the dining room, sit down at the table, and read the handwritten note Daddy left for me.

Good Morning, Baby girl,
I heard all about the wonderful day you had yesterday.
I am so proud of you and all that you've accomplished
since we've been here. You are a true winner! And I am
confident that you will be the best student council presi-
dent that school has ever seen. That's right! I've already
claimed it for you. Have a good day and I can't wait to
celebrate with you when I get home tonight!

Love, Daddy

Daddy's notes always make me smile. I open Corey's
next.

Hey Li'l Sis,
I knew you'd rock it. You're an Imes, after all. Now, it's
time for BH to find out what we already know and that's
how fly my li'l sis is. I have no doubt you won. Hit me on
the cellie or text me when you find out the official results!

Corey

I couldn't start my day without acknowledging the Man
Upstairs.

Dear God,
Today is the day. I hope I'm walking into a victory, but
even if I don't win, I've learned so much about myself in
the few months since moving to L.A. and going to Bea-
con Hills that it really doesn't matter whether I win the
election or not. I'm already a winner. I've learned the
true value of friendship, kindness, and honesty. I've also

learned not to worry so much. You've designed my life and it's special and filled with wonderful blessings and accomplishments that are meant just for me.

I didn't understand why I had to move here at first, but now I get it. Moving to Cali was about meeting new people and expanding my horizons. Living here has made me grow in ways I never imagined. Even though my crew is different and come from different walks of life, we've always got each other's backs when it's needed. I'm really happy, and I can finally say—and believe—that I truly belong here.

When I think about all I've experienced—swimming in my own pool, eating sushi (shrimp tempura rolls are good, but I'm still not feelin' the eel), becoming more confident, AND meeting T-Mac—I still can't believe it all. Even running for student council president was a big step, and I'm glad I took it. My one regret is that Maya and I aren't cool. Too bad she can't see beyond her crew of girls. But I can't worry about her. Maybe one day we'll become friends.

In some strange way, I feel like my being here even helped Deb deal with everything she's gone through. I proved to her—and myself—you don't have to be thin or change who you are to be beautiful and accepted. One day, I hope to make that statement on an even larger scale, maybe in front of a camera. I want people to understand that it's okay to be different, especially out here where image is everything.

Beacon Hills High
Study Guide

E boni Michelle Imes is a smart, confident young woman on the verge of high school. Full-figured and lovin' it, she and her girls, the TTC (Too Tight Crew), plan to do in high school what they did in middle school—run things!

It seems Eboni has her life all figured out until life throws her a curve that sends her entire family from Baltimore to Los Angeles for the most important four years of her life. Now, she doesn't know what to expect and that's got her worried.

The following questions are designed to spark a discussion that we hope will be compelling and thought-provoking. It is our desire that you learn valuable lessons from Eboni's experiences as you embark on your own life's journey.

* When we meet Eboni, she is a few days away from graduating from Saddleback Middle School. Though she's excited about graduation and what's next, she's also nervous about her new school. Why?

* Why are Eboni and Michelle friends?

* Describe Eboni's thoughts about going to high school. Can you relate? If so, how?

* At the mall, Eboni is at a loss for words when she spots her crush, Vincent Williams. Why?

* What does Michelle mean when she says to Eboni, "Hollywood is your dream, not mine. Things happen for a reason"?

* Eboni learned about talking to God from her grandmother, who taught her to talk to Him when she is going through personal trials. Discuss how Eboni applies this relationship to her life.

* What method do you use to get through challenges in your life?

* What do you think Eboni means when she says, after finding out that she has to move to Los Angeles, "God . . . why hast Thou forsaken me?"

* After landing in Los Angeles, what is Eboni's first impression of the city?

❋ When the Goldsteins introduce themselves, what is Eboni's first impression of Deb? Describe Deb's personality.

❋ Eboni meets Juan in Freshman English and she immediately notices that he is different by the way he acts and dresses. Do you have gay friends? If so, how did you feel when you found out they were gay?

❋ Eboni meets Robin in her favorite class, Debate. Why do they hit it off?

❋ Eboni is initially apprehensive about running for student council. Why?

❋ When Eboni sees star quarterback G Hicks, she thinks he is the finest guy since her Baltimore crush, Vincent, but she's too shy to speak to him. Can you relate to that feeling?

❋ When G finally acknowledges Eboni, he says he can tell she isn't from around here. What does he mean by that?

❋ At the Beverly Center, Deb and Eboni get into a deep discussion about weight issues. Deb thinks Eboni should diet with her. Eboni thinks Deb has gone overboard with the diets. Who do you think is right? Why?

❋ At Maya's birthday party, Eboni has another encounter with G, but he is called away by Maya before they can really talk. Why?

* When Eboni and Robin find Deb in the Red Room with Maya, the Sticks, and the football players, should they have busted up the party? If so, why? If not, why not?

* The morning after the party, Deb and Eboni have a girl talk about boys and sex. What does Deb mean when she says that as long as a boy doesn't "stick it in," then it's not sex? Do you agree or disagree?

* Discuss the definition of sex. Is oral sex considered sex?

* When Eboni finds out that Maya is going to be her opponent in the election, she has doubts about whether she can win. Why?

* When Mrs. Imes tells Eboni Mimmie's advice, "If you're gonna pray, then don't worry, and if you're gonna worry, then don't waste your time prayin'," in reference to the election, what does she mean?

* When Maya and her friends post a bogus rant on her MySpace page about Deb and Eboni, is Deb's idea to record Eboni's confrontation with Maya in the bathroom a good idea or a bad one?

* What does Eboni eventually learn from the bathroom incident?

* Eboni loves music in general, but singer T-Mac in particular. How does she use T-Mac's songs to help her deal with the ups and downs of life?

✱ Why was meeting T-Mac a turning point in her life?

✱ In Eboni's last talk with God, she says, "I didn't understand why I had to move here at first, but now I get it." What does she mean by that?

✱ What does Eboni eventually learn from her three new friends?

✱ What does Eboni learn about herself as a result of moving to Los Angeles? Describe three things that show her growth.